TEASE ME

A DRAGONS LOVE CURVES NOVEL

AIDY AWARD

FULFILL A DESTINY, SAVE THE WORLD,
AND THE SOUL OF HER MATE.

Fleur Anthousai, a curvy earth witch, has known since birth that she has a destiny to fulfill. Too bad nobody told her what it was. She hopes her friends, the Troika wolf pack of Rogue, New York, might have finally pointed her in the right direction when she's invited to the multi-pack mating ritual. Surely, becoming a wolf mate will set her on the path to understanding her own prophecy.
Steele Zeleny is a green warrior dragon and he's damn good at protecting the world from the darkness that is the demon dragons, all while romancing the pants off any and all the ladies. All bets are off when a shard of his soul demands that the curviest, sexiest little flower of a witch is his true mate. Something he was never supposed to have.

Fleur's destiny and Steele's soul are more important to the fate of the world than either of them know.

Copyright © 2018 by Aidy Award

Parts of this work were originally published as Sass Me, A Sassy Ever After Novella and Live For Me, a Dragons Love Curves short story Copyright © 2017 by Aidy Award

All rights reserved. No part of this publication may be reproduced, distributed or transmitted in any form or by any means, including photocopying, recording, or other electronic or mechanical methods, without the prior written permission of the publisher, except in the case of brief quotations embodied in critical reviews and certain other noncommercial uses permitted by copyright law. For permission requests, write to the publisher, addressed "Attention: Permissions Coordinator," at the address below.

Aidy Award /Coffee Break Publishing

www.coffeebreakpublishing.com

Publisher's Note: This is a work of fiction. Names, characters, places, and incidents are a product of the author's imagination. Locales and public names are sometimes used for atmospheric purposes. Any resemblance to actual people, living or dead, or to businesses, companies, events, institutions, or locales is completely coincidental.

Cover Design by Melody Simmons

Tease Me/ Aidy Award. -- 1st ed.

ISBN-13: 978-1-950228-99-7

*For my sister Sheri,
who might be part flower nymph too.*

You can call me Flower if you want to.

—Flower, Bambi

DUMB IDEA

This was the stupidest fucking idea ever. Skintight pants that tore off at the hips, nothing but suspenders above the waist, and a goddamn fireman's hat.

"Wooo hooo. Honey, take it off." A slightly older woman who was definitely the alpha female in the room whooped at them.

Steele leaned to the side to speak so only Daxton could hear. He fought to fake a smile for the ladies, but couldn't quite manage it, which was unusual. He'd always been able to charm the pants off any woman, anytime he liked.

His dragon wanted nothing to do with any of these ladies.

Weird.

The dragon part of him loved flirting, especially with beautiful women. Their soft luscious curves, the way they moaned when he licked them from head to toe, the way they came on his dick. Just not any of these screaming meamies.

"I'm going to kill you for talking me into wearing these costumes. You'll be a dragonskin rug in front of my fireplace come winter."

"You can murder me later. The Troika boys asked for our help. We might as well have some fun while we're doing it." Dax had his eyes on the rowdy red-head waving dollar bills like a lasso. He always did go for the brash and bawdy types.

Two minutes after they'd walked into Sleepy Folk Speakeasy, Konstantin Troika jumped at the chance of having two dragon warriors around. A pre-mating party, he'd called it, and promised a room full of horny women, who didn't need to know they were being guarded.

Steele didn't mind protecting the women while on his R&R. Combining work hard and play hard together was his specialty.

The Troika boys wanted the unmated women who were here for the special three-pack mating get together to have extra security. They just didn't want their mates knowing about it.

What Kosta hadn't said was that Steele and Dax were the entertainment.

Thank the First Dragon, Dax stepped forward and into the crowd of women all stuffed into this snack-sized apartment. They surrounded him with hoots and hollers sounding to him more like a pack of wolves than humans. At least half of them were shifter she-wolves, anyway.

Two women grabbed Steele's arms and pulled him into their circle, sliding their bodies up and down his, running their hands over his bare chest. Their touches did nothing for him but send a few creepy crawlies up his skin.

What the hell was wrong with him? This was the perfect opportunity. Beautiful women were literally begging him to take his clothes off, and he couldn't be less interested.

Steele had every intention of getting laid at least a couple dozen times on his week off, but maybe not all on the same night. These women were crazy and weren't doing it for him at all.

That worried him. He hadn't been turned off since he'd hit puberty. These last few years a fucking houseplant could turn him on.

Was his Prime creeping up on him already?

No way. He wouldn't let it. A deep beat coupled with a tinny *psst psst psst* blared from the cheap portable stereo. He could shake his ass with the best of them. Time to get his flirt on.

Steele grabbed the closest woman at the hips and lifted her, wrapping her legs around his waist. He ground against her, hoping, waiting for his cock to join the god-damned party.

"Go, Zara, go, Zara." The women around him chanted and the lady in his arms turned firetruck red.

"Niko is going to go ballistic when he hears about this," she squealed.

"Good. A little jealousy will go a long way." The other woman dancing at his side, tried to grab his ass and laughed. "I love it when Max gets all possessive, the sex is amazing. So, me next."

Kosta had been right. These women were trouble with a capital T-R-O-U-B-L and E. He was down for having a good time, but he would never come between anyone and their mate. He danced with them for another minute and then spun both around and into a waiting couch. "Now, now ladies. Let the single girls have a chance, too."

"Spoilsport." Max's mate folded her arms and pouted.

This party should be exactly what he needed, but tonight

Steele would rather wrap himself around one soft cuddly woman. One who could warm his bed during the long winter months at his post at the Green Wyr stronghold.

The Czech winter was coming, and he didn't want to spend it alone.

Pretending to be strippers at a pre-mating party was not the way to find a mate.

Wait. Whoa, hold the phone. Mate? No fucking way.

Just because Jakob Zeleny, the head of his Wyr clan was the first dragon in more than six-hundred years to find a true mate didn't mean the rest of them would, or could, or even should.

Nope. Steele was on the verge of hitting his Prime years. His glory days of carousing and bedding every woman he could would end too soon. He had to take every advantage of this vacation to get into as many dirty girl's panties as possible.

A goddess in a pink flowy top and tight jeans that hugged all her curves - and there were oh so many - walked into the room with a tray of drinks.

His eyes were instantly drawn to the green sparkling tree charm hanging from a chain just above her fantastic tits. He'd happily add both the charm and this hot curvy chick to his treasure trove. He tore his eyes from the necklace and drew his gaze down to the sweet sway of her hips and over her plump ass.

Fuck, yeah. Those were the exact panties he aimed to get into. He danced his way out of the group of women and over to his pink prey. She stopped beside him not attempting to take the cocktails into the pulsing crowd of women now surrounding Dax.

"Having fun, big boy?" A soft voice that sounded like ripe peaches, a warm mountain sunrise, and butterfly wings lilted from her.

What the fuck did that even mean? He shook his head waiting for the momentary brain fart to pass.

"No?" She laughed, the sound tinkling like frozen bluebells.

Holy shit. His brain was broken.

He licked his lips and tried to speak. A low growl came out.

"Whoa. Sorry. I didn't know we paid for Grumpy Bear."

He was no bear. But she wasn't either. Her green eyes danced for him and sparkled brighter than her jewelry. They were the exact color of the field in front of his cabin in the spring after a rainstorm.

This was a wolf party, he inhaled her sweet scent looking for the nature of her shifter animal. She wasn't one of the wolves, but she wasn't a mere human. He stared into her eyes, searching for any clue, scenting her light arousal, trying to figure out what form she would take.

A fluffy bunny or a lovely plump doe. She had a soft look about her that he liked, but she was a little too smart-ass to be a carrot-eater. They were all gentle. She had a bite. Her scent teased all his senses.

A skunk maybe. Soft and docile, but also clever and ravenous.

He uncrossed his arms and shook them out. "No, little flower, you didn't pay for a grump, and I'm no bear."

"That I can see." She looked him up and down, taking her time, damn well drinking him in.

Oh, she had to be a hunter with that needy glint to her eye.

He'd just been made into a piece of meat to her, he was positive of that. If he didn't know better he'd say she was part dragon.

But there was no such thing as a female dragon.

"And if you didn't notice. I'm not exactly little." There was both a bit of defiance and something else shy in her voice and eyes.

Yeah. He'd noticed. She had nice wide hips he could grab onto while he thrust into her, a thick ass he couldn't wait to squeeze, and plump tits he could get lost in for years.

Shit. He'd been too long without a woman. He'd gone from hello to growl to imagining fucking her brains out all inside of a minute. Well, minus the hello.

"I noticed every luscious inch of you, Flower."

Her eyes widened and she laughed, more than the tinkling giggle from before. This was hearty from the gut. The sound went straight into his balls and lifted his cock.

About time it fucking showed up.

"Do we have to pay extra for the fake flirtations or is that part of the service?"

Apparently he needed to up his game. "It wasn't fake. You're a beautifully fuckable woman I'd like to lick up and down until you're screaming from the pleasure."

There. That ought to do it.

She got the cutest crinkle between her eyes, blinked and shook her head like he'd said the most ridiculous thing she'd ever heard. Then she raised the tray of drinks and walked into the crowd.

"Okay, ladies. Who wants some of Galyna's marshmallow shots?" She tossed the words out, not giving him another look.

Every scale-covered fiber of his dragon-being wanted, no needed, to follow her. He wasn't one to go against his dragon. Two steps forward and he was surrounded by three women who undulated and ground themselves against him.

"Oh my gawd. Look at these muscles," one woman said, pawing at his stomach.

"And those arms." Another woman lifted his elbow and caressed his bicep. "Flex it for me."

His Flower was smiling and chatting, handing out drinks, and rolls of dollar bills to the twenty some-odd women. If he could just escape these fondlers he'd push through, take her away from all this, and get to know her. In a biblical sense.

He didn't know her name and couldn't call to her. He bid her to look at him with his will. He was so damn close to calling up his dragon form, so he could simply speak into her mind.

She must have felt him staring at her because she looked up from her conversation. "I'm not paying you to stand around, grumpy. Shake that ass."

"What a tight ass it is." One of the fondlers ran a hand over his rear and pinched it.

He almost yelped. Holy crap. He was no sensitive-skinned baby, but damn. He was going to have a welt. These she-wolves were aggressive. Not that he minded a woman who went after what she wanted. Especially if *he* was what she wanted.

What he wanted right now was the pink bit of flesh peeking between Flower's shirt and her jeans as she bent over to set her tray on the table.

Oh, how he could bend her over that table.

He scooted away from pincher-lady, who must be a damn crab-shifter, and tried to get closer to Flower.

"Take it off, fireman. Let's see your hose." The Velcro holding his pants together pulled, almost coming apart as the women clawed at him.

He pushed their hands away, his only focus on getting to his lady in pink. She handed out the last of her drinks, slid around the back of the couch, and circled around the group going back to the kitchen.

He stalked her movement with his eyes, loving the chase, and the slippery way she kept evading him. "You ladies are wearing me out. I think I need a drink."

Half a dozen women held up shot glasses made from marshmallows for him.

"Uh, thanks, but I'll grab some water." Steele followed his prey, into the soft light of the kitchen. Every counter top was covered in rows of herbs and greenery. More baskets hung over the sink and in the window.

He'd left an apartment living room and entered a forest of edible greens. It was stunning, and his dragon reveled in the earthy scent of it all. She might really be a bunny shifter. One that he was going to hunt down and eat. In the fun way.

His Flower stood with her back to him, arranging cups of blue, red, and purple gloop on her tray. Finally, he had her alone.

"What is your name, little flower?

She jumped about three feet. "You scared me. Don't you know not to sneak up on a girl like that?" She downed one of the shots of goo, and then offered one to him. "I'm Fleur. I assumed you knew from the agency. I booked the strippers, I thought maybe my name was down as a contact or something."

He took her hand, set the cup down, and kissed her palm, then her wrist. A zing zipped through his lips, down his spine and straight to his cock.

"Oh, you shocked me." She giggled, but didn't pull her hand away.

He continued kissing up her arm, and then to her neck, touching the chain of the necklace. It glinted, calling to him. He licked the gold and her skin below.

"I don't know what you're doing or why you're doing it to me, but it feels amazing, don't stop." Fleur pushed her hands into his hair and gripped his scalp, urging him on.

Good thing these pants were tear away Velcro, because he wouldn't be able to wait very long to get inside her heat. He could scent the spike in her arousal. It pushed his own even higher.

She tilted her head to the side, giving him even more access. "If you didn't already know my name, why do you keep calling me flower?"

He nibbled his way up to her ear, then whispered, "Have you ever seen Bambi?"

"Sure." She sucked in a surprised breath and pushed him away. Her eyes got wide and then narrowed. "Oh my Gods. Is this your polite stripper way of telling me I smell? As in skunky?"

He laughed deep and hard. "No. In fact, you smell like springtime, and harvest, and green valleys, and snow-capped mountains."

"Wow. You are such a flirt. That agency rocks. I'll remember to request you for next year's pre-mating party.

Although, I'll get a bit green, but you have got to kiss some of the other single girls here like that. Big tips will definitely get shoved down your pants. In fact, you should check with Zara to see if she can get you a job at The Sleepy Folk. With your flirting skills you'd get lots of tips from all the cougars."

He may not ever put his lips on another woman's flesh ever again. "I am not flirting with you. I am seducing you."

"Do you get a bonus if we request you by name? What's your name? Ooh, wait, do guys have stripper names, too? I'll bet yours is cinnamon, no wait, honey buns."

"I don't belong to any agency, I don't need a job, and I'm not a stripper. My name is Steele."

"That's a perfect stripper name. Wait. You're not from the agency? Are you freelance? I didn't know that was a thing."

Steele stepped closer, pushing her lush body against the counter. He set a hand on either side, caging her in.

"I am not a stripper, little flower. I am a dragon."

DID HE SAY DRAGON?

Fleur knew lots of shape-shifters. She'd become friends with Zara and Galyna when she'd started working at the community center. They'd fully embraced her educational gardening project.

The Troika's had become almost a second family to her. Well, a first family, since she didn't really have one. Zara, Galyna, and Heli hadn't thought she was a complete weirdo like everyone else at her former jobs… or life.

She'd had more than a passing crush on at least two or three of the Troika boys when the girls had introduced her to them. But they were all paired off with her friends, mated.

The sex-on-a-stick standing in front of her was not mate material. What he was, was the hottest thing she'd ever seen and she tried her best to convince herself his flirting was the cause of her instant attraction to him.

She didn't get a whole lot of action from most guys. They couldn't see past her chubby cheeks and butt. It was fun to pretend he thought she was all that and a bag of salt and vinegar chips.

"A dragon, huh?" She shrugged like it was no big deal. In all her time in Rogue, New York, she'd never once known a dragon. There weren't many in the States at all. Were all of them this charismatic and sexy? Maybe it was that delicious European accent of his.

He ran the back of his knuckles down her arm. "Yes, Daxton and I are both dragon shifters. But what are you, my treasure?"

While she was thoroughly enjoying all the attention this dominant, alpha shifter was showing her, she had other plans. Fleur poked him in the chest, giving herself a little static electricity shock, pushing him away. "Don't go thinking you can eat me up. I've got a party to hostess and Jell-O shots to hand out."

Plus, there was this year's mating ritual, the biggest one ever, three packs from across the country were coming together. Selena Troika, the matriarch of the pack had invited her, and while the girls warned her about Selena's matchmaking, Fleur was excited.

Steele didn't budge an inch when she tried to push him away. He did get a lascivious glint to his eye. "I will do everything in my power to eat you up. And down, and sideways if you like."

His tongue poked out and he licked his lips, then bit the lower one. The look on his face wasn't a grin. No, it was unadulterated sizzling sin.

A flutter tickled her low in the belly. She couldn't help the smile flirting with this dragon brought to her lips. He was a total perv, and she kinda liked that. Not a lot of men she'd known had found her perv-worthy.

She'd let him flirt and tease her with little kisses when she thought he was a stripper, thinking that zing she'd felt was part of the excitement of the night.

But if he was a shifter, then she needed to keep her distance. The mating ritual was tomorrow night. If she was lucky, she'd smell *delicioso* to one of the wolves and he'd choose her to be his mate.

She was destined to mate a wolf. Maybe. Hopefully.

Fleur had no idea what her destiny was, only that she had one. Her mother had told her so her entire life. Told her to prepare for it, save herself for it, while never even eluding to what she should prepare for. It made her feel stuck. Fleur had held herself back from doing so many things in her life, waiting for that destiny to show up.

Now it was here.

Probably.

Not like she could ask her mom anyway. Her mother was currently spending the summer as a red windflower at the burial site of Fleur's father. Again.

Tonight, having fun with all the other women destined for the mating ritual out there living it up, she wanted to have fun, too.

Whatever was supposed to happen to her could wait for one more night. This might be the last time she could ever do something naughty.

She wanted so badly for her life to change, to stop waiting and get to the exciting part. Maybe that would happen tomorrow night, or maybe this was it, the beginning of a new adventurous life for her. Right here in her own kitchen.

Yeah. It was. She decided.

A tingling in her heart, directly behind the Tree of Hesperides pendant she wore told her to follow that instinct.

She usually ignored those kinds of feelings, because what if they were pulling her away from her destiny? For once, she was going to let loose. Some hot and heavy making out was exactly what the herbalist ordered.

His skin was oh, so touchable. She dragged her finger from the base of his neck to between his pecs. "You're dirty, dragon."

He chuckled. "You have no idea."

"Show me." Fleur grabbed him behind the neck and pulled him in for a kiss.

What a kiss it was. He practically inhaled her, spearing his hands into her hair to hold her close. Their tongues dueled, slashing at each other. Steele tasted like warm mint, fresh and bright. Not the toothpaste kind, but like the real fresh leaves. She couldn't get enough.

He slid one hand all the way down her arm, over her hip, and to her butt. She's always thought her rear end was too big, but the way he kneaded and squeezed, it was currently her favorite body part.

"Fuck, Fleur. I want to rip your clothes right off you." He grabbed the back of her thigh and lifted it, wrapping her leg over his hip.

It took her a second to register what he said, with the way his hand was pushing up underneath the hem of her shirt. "No, no, don't do that. There are a dozen people ten feet away in the other room."

She wanted adventure, not exhibitionism.

He growled and lifted her other leg, spreading her open. He pushed his hips forward, thrusting against her, sending stars shooting through her vision.

Oh, gods and goddesses. She could see how he got his name. Whatever he was hiding behind those pants, rocking against her in all the right places was definitely made of steel, or kryptonite.

Because, she was feeling weaker by the second. Very much more of this and she'd be begging him to strip her clothes off. This was so delectably naughty, and so much hotter than any other sexy times she'd ever had. They weren't even having sex. Yet.

Her legs acted of their own volition and pulled him in closer. She had no control over her body at the moment. It was doing whatever it wanted. Namely Steele.

She couldn't think straight, not with the way his touch had her body in overdrive. Even in her naughtiest fantasies about mating a wolf-shifter, she hadn't come close to losing her mind to lust like this.

"Your kiss is driving me crazy. I'll never get enough of you." Steele growled against her and licked his way across her bottom lip.

She was driving him crazy? She was the one whose body and mind were doing the opposite of everything she'd ever been taught.

Steele's kisses went straight to her core and she wanted more, so much more. She didn't even care that he was probably giving her a line. One tiny minute in his arms and already her panties were soaked.

She'd never reacted to any man, or wolf, this way. Even her vibrator didn't make her this hot and needy. Where was a bed and a condom when she needed it?

Good Gods. This wasn't meant to be more than a flirtatious make out session. First base, maybe second. Here they were rounding third and her body was chanting home, home, home.

It was too fast. She wanted a little fun, not a one-night stand. Fleur knew better than to let go like this. She'd been warned about allowing herself to play these kinds of games. Especially since this wasn't her destined mate pushing against the wall and closer to orgasm. Enough. "Steele, we have to slow down."

He nipped at the skin of her neck, sending an earthquake with shockwaves through her whole body.

Mmm, yes, his mouth on her neck felt amazing. "Never mind. No, we don't, forget I said anything. Do that bitey thing again."

He scraped his teeth across her skin, right above her collarbone, and she whimpered with the pleasure of it. She wanted him to bite her, mark her with his teeth.

Why would she want that? "Steele, please, I need…"

She didn't know what she needed. Her mind was fritzing. Her body and her libido had totally taken control now.

"Yes, little flower, I need you, too. Where is your bedroom? We'll lock the door, and I'll make you come all night long."

Great idea.

No. No, it wasn't. Fleur wasn't thinking straight, or at all. She'd met this guy less than an hour ago. She didn't know what kind of person he was, where he was from, or anything. All she knew was how she'd been instantly attracted to him and was supposed to push those feelings down like she always did.

She wasn't thinking. She was feeling, and it was freeing.

Too much so. She wasn't free. She had a destiny.

There was no way a dragon she'd only met tonight was that destiny.

Cheering came from the living room and then a series of boos. The ruckus was enough to bring Fleur back to the present, remembering who and where she was, what and how she was meant to behave.

This wasn't it.

"Steele, stop." She pushed against his head, still glued to her neck.

The loss of his lips against her skin quite literally hurt.

"What's wrong, babe?" He tilted his head to the side and rubbed her back. "Did I do something you don't like? I'll learn your body and what you need as fast as I can. I promise."

His eyes twinkled with need and even in the heat of their make-out passion he was being sweet and sensitive to her needs. Fleur almost gave in. No one's eyes had ever glowed for her, not like this.

Sigh. "We can't do this."

He nuzzled her neck and whispered into her ear. "Do what? Have sex on the countertop? I'll carry you to your bed."

Yeah, right.

"Don't be ridiculous, you can't carry me. And no, I mean this." She waved her hand between the two of them.

He lifted her into his arms and took several steps across the room. "I can carry you, and I will. Where is your bedroom, my sweet?"

Fleur's fear of breaking him and her ass when he dropped her spiked like a flowering cactus, poking her from the inside out.

"Holy basil. Put me down before you drop me." She flailed until he set her feet back on the floor.

"I liked having you in my arms, but if you don't, I'll get over it, as long I can have you in my arms like this." He pulled her to him and gently kissed her.

He'd gone from raging need to sweet and gentle in the blink of an eye, and she wanted him even more for that. Just one more kiss and then she'd be satisfied.

"Whoa, sorry. Covering my eyes. Sorry." Zara's voice broke through the thick need in Fleur's brain. "But I'm not sure you should be macking on this guy. The two of them aren't even strippers."

Double sigh. "I know. They're dragons, or at least this one is."

Fleur stepped out of Steele's arms and straightened her top. He moved beside her, and put a hand on her lower back, all possessive-like.

That felt entirely too good.

Zara threw her hands up in the air. "What? We all thought they were just strippers. Why didn't you tell us? Did my mate put you up to this."

She jerked her thumb in her dragon's direction. Uh, no, she shook her head. The dragon, a dragon, not her dragon. "No, of course not. I just found out a minute ago Steele here was a dragon shifter."

Heli popped into the kitchen giving Steele the stink-eye. "My stupid over protective man-child, oh, I mean mate, sent them. I'm sure he thought they'd be safer than strangers or something dumb like that."

Galyna joined them and she did not look happy either. Although, when Selena came in she looked more humored than mad.

"Kosta put you up to this?" Galyna asked, glaring at Steele

and folding her arms across her chest, tapping her foot. She tapped it any harder and there would be a hole in the linoleum floor before long.

"Uh, yeah." Steele lifted an arm and rubbed behind his neck.

"You're not strippers?" Galyna, who was the least violent of the bunch had daggers coming out of her eyes.

He addressed Fleur with the save-me-from-your-angry-friends look on his face. "I *am* a dragon, and I did tell you I was not a stripper."

"Strippers or not, you two can get the hell out of our party," Zara said.

Galyna poked Steele in the chest. "And tell Kosta he will have to find another way to rain on our parade."

"Yeah." A resounding chorus came from the rest of the ladies.

Fleur bit the inside of her lip to keep from laughing. Her friends were so damn serious, but she thought it was cute and hilarious that the men had tried to keep their women in check by sending these unsuspecting dragons to the pre-mating party. She wasn't disappointed in the least at the choice Kosta had made.

"Those fools never liked the idea of this party in the first place. So, I say we make it a tradition," Zara said.

Jules came into the kitchen leading Daxton by his ear. The dragon actually looked like he was having fun. "Hey, ladies. I swear, Kosta said this was a party with a bunch of horny women. That was it. Except the part where he said not to touch any of you five, and asked me to report back to him what went on here and to make sure you didn't get into any trouble."

Heli rubbed her hands together. "Oh, he is getting his ass kicked when I get home. He is not allowed to spoil our fun."

"Now girls, don't be too hard on your mates." Selena was barely keeping a chuckle out of her voice. "Kosta was simply doing as I told him to."

"Selena. This whole bachelorette-style party was your idea in the first place. Why would you help our mates sabotage it?" Zara looked genuinely confused.

Fleur felt the same. Selena was the coolest mom-figure she knew, and she was a certified matchmaker, with a dash of trouble thrown in. It didn't seem in line with her usual plans to keep any potential mate from getting their flirt on.

"The dragons weren't here for you married girls, were they?" Selena winked at Fleur. "Besides, which one of you isn't quite sure you're getting ravished when you get home just so your mates can get the scent of these delicious young dragons off you?"

While Zara had a look of embarrassed shock on her face, the other girls' expressions went from angry to downright dirty.

Fleur cleared her throat to keep from laughing out loud. She couldn't wait to join in the shenanigans of having a wolf mate of her own. Then maybe she'd feel like a real part of the family and not so much the third-wheel single cousin.

She gave Steele a shove toward the hallway. He didn't move even a centimeter. "You two better get on out of here. Send our regards to the Troika boys."

"I'm not going anywhere, little flower." He bent and whispered in her ear, "Unless it's to your bedroom."

Fleur was sure her face and neck had just gone the color of

a whole damn field of poppies. She turned her back on Steele and gave the other dragon a shove instead.

A low growl came from behind her, but it stopped the second she took her hands off.

Daxton shrugged and went toward the door of his own accord. Of course, he was probably trying to avoid getting his ear torn off by Jules. "Come on, Steele. Our cover is blown. Gonna have to get lucky somewhere else."

The women surrounded both men and shoved them toward the door. Right before Zara slammed it on them, Steele pointed at Fleur.

"I'll be back for you, little flower."

PROTECT HER OR DIE

"Dragon's fire, I thought those she-wolves were going to eat my face off." Daxton laughed and opened up the back of the rented SUV. He pulled out the pile of clothes they'd left back there.

Steele grabbed his shirt and jeans. The less time he had to spend in these ridiculous pants the better. "What the hell did you say to them to piss them off like that?"

"Only that I was damn grateful to Kosta for sending us over. That's when they flipped their shit."

Steele riffled through one of the pockets to find his soul shard. He'd felt uncomfortable leaving the most important thing he owned in the car. But it would have been even worse to allow it to be manhandled by all those women. "Then I don't know whether to blame you or Kosta for losing my shot with Fleur tonight."

"That curvy chick you were practically fucking in the kitchen? She's was a hot piece of ass. I wouldn't mind getting some of that action."

Steele grabbed Dax by the throat and threw him up against

the side of the car. Both of their dragons rose to the surface, ready for a fight. Steele snarled. "Don't even think about her in that way. She is mine."

Dax glared at him, studying his face. Then he raised his hands, surrendering. "Holy shit. Fine, you've got dibs. I was way more into the redhead anyway."

Steele released Dax, surprised at his own vehemence. It wasn't like he couldn't get any number of women he wanted. She was just another woman.

His gut clenched at the thought. Fuck that. She was a hell of a lot more. He didn't know why, but she was.

He snatched at his shirt and pulled it over his head. The material felt rough against his skin. Nothing like Fleur's soft lips. The stupid fireman pants went into a pile, and he pulled on his jeans.

Dax did the same, and slipped the cord with his red soul shard over his head. It glinted briefly, its internal fire shining for a brief moment when it settled against Dax's skin.

Steele reached into his pocket and pulled his own soul shard out, anxious to reconnect with the gift from the White Witch that allowed him to shift from man to dragon. It blazed like a lighthouse beacon into the night, filling the darkness with its green light.

He and Dax stared at the green crystal-like talisman. "What the fuck, dude?"

What the fuck, indeed. Had something happened to his shard while they'd been dicking around? He'd never seen any dragon's shard do anything but hang around their necks and occasionally glow with a bit of colored light.

Steele put the pendant on and tucked it under his shirt.

The second it hit his skin a pleasure-pain shot through him, so great it brought him to his knees with its power.

He cried out and grabbed at the bumper of the SUV to steady himself. He crushed the metal in his fist, his claws extending from the ends of his fingers. His dragon shimmered across his skin, stretching, pushing its way out.

The beast part of him wrenched control and roared into the night, taking him fully into the shift. He clawed at the ground, reveling in the new power pouring through him.

Then as suddenly as it had taken him over, the power faded and the dragon receded, leaving Steele in his human form, gasping for air.

"Well, we're not getting the deposit back on the rental, that's for sure." Dax stared at Steele, crouched in a fighting-ready stance. He glanced to the right then back.

The SUV lay upside-down, it's windows shattered, and the bumper ripped clean off.

"You want to tell me what the hell just happened?"

"I...don't know." The shard at his chest faded to a soft glow, like the light from a firefly, and warmed his skin beneath it.

Dax's voice dropped low and his red scales flickered across his skin. "Can you stand? Can you fight?"

Steele got to his feet. "Yeah. I can. Why?"

"Because we've got company." Dax growled and jerked his chin to the shadows building around them. Danger brewed in that darkness. Damn it. This was supposed to be a vacation.

Dax didn't wait and shifted into his dragon.

The shadows grew and formed into the shape of half a dozen black winged creatures, like Steele's own form, only twisted and dark.

Demon dragons.

What the hell were they doing here?

Steele called his dragon back up, the transformation moving through him faster and easier. The world around him shrank as he shifted, his dragon form grew larger than ever before. He roared at the black demon dragons approaching. Power flowed through him, waiting for him to call upon it to battle these disgusting blights on the world.

The snakelike creatures with their sooty scales and wings were pure evil. They came from the darkness to spread plague and chaos on the world and it was every dragon warrior's job to send them back to hell.

He and Dax had trained and fought together in many battles. They could work together on instinct. They'd need all their skills to defeat the demon dragons amassing around them. It might be two against ten, but Steele would still put the odds in his favor. He was twice the size of any of them, maybe more now, and Dax was ruthless when it came to killing demon dragons.

The black death moved as a unit, coordinated in their attack, surrounding them on three sides.

Dax breathed out a swath of fire, stymying the demon's first attempt to get to the two of them. They were not dissuaded and one spit its black smoke and fire back at Dax while its kin jumped together to attack Steele on two sides.

Steele struck out, swinging his tail in a wide arc, making contact with half the beasts around them, sending the things careening and crashing. One hit a tree and the other slammed into the nearest building.

Fleur's building.

Steele sent out a prayer to the First Dragon that the

women would continue their party inside and not have a clue how close death had come to their door.

The demon dragons would devour a pretty plump thing like Fleur. She'd be defenseless against them.

He could never let that happen. Every protective instinct flared inside like fire, and he lashed at the demon dragons, shredding those nearest to him.

A half-dozen black oily stains smeared the street and sidewalk in moments as he cut them down and tore out their throats. With each kill his soul shard grew brighter, as if declaring his victory.

Two new demon dragons appeared from the darkness and screeched at their remaining comrades. They stayed back from the fray while the others turned and focused their attack on Dax.

Cowards.

Dax sliced at two of them, but before he could destroy them, the other two piled on top, taking him to the ground. Steele roared, and used all his might to pounce on the bastards, snapping at them with his teeth and tearing at their skin.

His friend was at the bottom of the pile, but holding his own. Steele could feel the heat from Dax's fire burning the demons from underneath. He speared one demon through the chest with his claw, tossing it at the cowards standing in the shadow of Fleur's building.

Three more to go.

He reached into the fracas to grab another beast. Two sets of claws dug into him from behind, ripping at his shoulders, gripping the cord of his soul shard.

Steele bucked and rolled, but he couldn't throw them off.

The more he fought them, the harder they held on. The cord was strong but not unbreakable.

"Steele, Dax, look out." Fleur and six of the she-wolves stood at the entrance to the building watching wide-eyed as the battle on the street raged.

His shard lit up the area with its green light, growing stronger by the second. Steele rolled, trying to crush the demon dragons beneath his giant body, or at least pin them to the ground.

"*No, Fleur. Get back, get inside.*" Steele projected his plea into her mind. He should have gone back in to protect her from these bastards.

Three of the women around Fleur shifted into snarling wolves and joined the battle, ripping and clawing at the remaining demons.

The other three guarded Fleur and the entrance to the building. The one called Zara even had a large rifle at the ready.

He sure hoped she knew how to use it and didn't shoot him in the process.

One of the demons jumped off his back, shredding the skin and scales at his neck, slicing through the shard's cord with his razor claws.

Something deep inside Steele's chest tore when the shard fell from his skin. For a moment, he lost his breath from the pain of it. His fight was gone, and he fell out of his dragon form, the shift washing over him and out of his control.

The demon dragon held the glowing shard, a piece of Steele's own soul in his fist, mesmerized by its light, drooling and snarling over its new treasure. Steele reached for the light, but he was weak now, and losing more strength by the second.

Dax and the wolves battled the remaining demon dragons until they were destroyed and only the bastard holding Steele's shard remained.

It was outnumbered, and it knew it.

The wolves and Dax could stop it. They had to.

The demon dragon spread its wings, and while it couldn't fly, it could leap, which is exactly what it did.

Three feet into the air, the trees lining the streets came alive and stretched their branches blocking its path. It smashed through one tree, only to be smacked down by another.

The light from the shard intensified so bright, it was matched only by another light coming from the entrance to the building.

The necklace around Fleur's neck glowed with the same light. She had her eyes closed and her hands raised. Fleur controlled the trees. With a swish of her arms they followed her directions.

Each movement by the demon dragon was met by an increase in the light from her necklace and his shard, plus a literal beating from the growth of new branches on the trees.

The demon dragon screeched and dove away from the angry orchard and straight at Fleur.

"Fleur, no." Steele yelled and found his last bit of strength. He ran and jumped, collided with the demon dragon in mid-air, rolling to the ground at Fleur's feet. Steele lifted his legs and double barrel kicked the demon away from Fleur.

The demon dragon moved back only a little and lashed out at Steele. It was much bigger than he was now and easily threw him into the entrance where the women stood. The beast had torn his human flesh, ripping his chest open.

He slid down the door and onto his back leaving a streak of blood behind him. He'd happily give his life, his short 150 years, to have saved Fleur.

But there would be no dying this day. Until the final demon dragon was defeated, he would protect Fleur.

For reasons he could not explain, his only focus was to make sure she was unharmed. He didn't understand the feelings driving him to keep her safe, he only obeyed them with all of his might.

He couldn't feel any pain. His limbs wouldn't work, no matter how his mind yelled at them to get up, to defend Fleur. He swallowed and blood bubbled from his lips.

He heard the crack of bones as the remaining women shifted. Before his next ragged breath, they'd ripped the demon dragon's throat out. It dissolved into smoke, dropping the soul shard.

Fleur snagged it from the ground. The night lit up even brighter than before, turning the dark into a brilliant green day. He felt the shard's power skim over his soul, and a new knowledge flowed through him.

His beautiful Fleur.

All he could do was stare up at the beauty that was his true mate.

His true mate.

A gift from the First Dragon.

She knelt beside him, pushed his tattered clothing aside, and assessed his wounds. "Dear Gods of Olympus. You're bleeding everywhere."

He tried to smile, to soothe her from the coming pain. "I'm

sorry, little flower. Please forgive me."

She ripped his shirt, pressing the bundle of cloth over the bloodiest of his wounds. "For bleeding? I don't think you can help that." She wiped her arm across her forehead, pushing the hair out of her eyes, but leaving a streak of his blood. "Don't worry, help will be here soon. Selena called her family. The Troika men and the enforcers will be here any minute."

Mine. His dragon clawed from inside, needing to claim his mate, needing to be reassured she hadn't been harmed or tainted by the demon dragons.

But even the power of the most feral, animalistic part of his being withered. Some piece of him he hadn't even known existed until tonight, was missing.

"No, little flower. For leaving you when we've only come together."

He expected tears from her, but he got narrowed eyes glaring down at him instead. "Oh no you don't."

He hadn't even properly claimed her, hadn't marked her as his. One final kiss from her would have to be enough, but his lips and tongue weren't working.

No, damn it. He couldn't leave her. She was his to love and protect. The very depths of his core screamed out, reaching for her.

His vision faded, tunneling until all he saw was her pretty face.

How could he protect her from the demon dragons, from anything in her world that might hurt her, if he died? First Dragon, hear his plea. Don't let him leave her alone and in danger.

The tunnel tightened to only her eyes, glowing for him, and finally darkness.

SAVE THE DRAGON

Fleur smacked Steele's cheeks, trying to get him to open his eyes. She wasn't sure how or why, but she could feel the life draining out of him by the second. It felt like it was draining her, too.

"Someone call an ambulance," she yelled, but there was no way even the best first responders would know how to save a dragon. Fear for his life and a need to help him bubbled inside of her chest, smoky and hot.

Humans didn't even know about shifters. Their doctors wouldn't be able to help and Fleur would have let a secret kept for millennia out. She didn't care. She had to save Steele.

Dax, ran over and slid to her side. "Damn, damn. Why doesn't he shift and heal himself?"

"Can you help him? I don't know what to do." The light from the green crystal the black dragon-lizard thing dropped was fading, too.

He shook his head. "I'm a red dragon, not a green. I can't heal. He was supposed to save my sorry ass if anything happened to us." He shook Steele's shoulder. "Come on, man, shift."

Galyna appeared with her in-case-of-emergency-werewolfing bag and handed out clothes to the women who had shifted back to human form and a blanket for Steele. "Here, I'm sorry. I don't think I have anything else that can help."

Fleur kept one hand on his wound, keeping the pressure on, and spread the blanket over him with the other. If she could keep him warm until she figured out how to help him heal, he would have a better chance.

She swallowed down the acrid taste in the back of her throat. No way a blanket would be enough. She knew basic first aid, and could treat all kinds of illnesses with her medicinal garden, but she had to figure out another way to help him. Think, think.

The rest of the women joined them, all in various states of disrepair, clothing torn, scratches and bruises all over their bodies.

"Hey, how come you guys are fully clothed and we're over here in shreds?" Zara asked Dax.

"Our shift isn't like yours. We were gifted the power to move between forms by the White Witch, mate to the First Dragon. The magic allows us to keep our forms, our possessions, and our clothing."

"I need to make friends with this witch. I go through clothes like there's no tomorrow," Jules said.

"Unfortunately, she died about seven-hundred years ago. So, I don't think that is possible." Dax waved the girls' questions off and touched Fleur's shoulder. "Can you help him?"

"Do you want me to run up and get some of your herbs or

the salves? The one you made for my sunburn worked like a miracle. Would they help?" Galyna asked.

"Yes. No. I don't know. They're for minor first aid, like bug bites and PMS, not for sucking chest wounds."

Did she have anything on hand that could stop the bleeding? She did have some wild iris root. That would help with bleeding, but not this much.

"What the fuck happened? Heli, Mom are you okay?" Kosta pushed his way into the circle of women and gathered Heli into his arms.

"I'm fine. But this guy isn't." Heli pointed down at Steele.

Her assessment of Steele's wounds tore at Fleur's gut. Heli was right. He really wasn't fine. He was dying, and she didn't have any way to stop it.

She'd only just met him like an hour ago, and she didn't understand why, but she could not lose him. Something inside her would break if he died.

"*Dirmo.*" Kosta swore in Russian and shook his head.

Niko shoved in and grabbed Zara, kissing her hard and then looking her up and down. "Those don't look like wolves' claw marks. What attacked you all?"

"Some sort of black lizard men. I guess they were dragons, but nothing like these two." Zara snuggled against Niko.

"Black dragons? What the hell? Did you guys bring some sort of feud with you?" Niko's voice turned dark, the alpha in him coming out.

Fleur wished they'd all shut up and let her think. Yarrow root? No. She didn't have time to make a poultice and didn't know what she'd do with it anyway. Not like she could pour it straight into his gaping wounds. No. What she needed was a god-damned needle and a whole spool of thread.

Dax stood and shook his head. "They shouldn't be here. I've never heard of demon dragons in this area. That's what they are, part demon, part dragon, and all evil."

Niko growled and paced, circling Zara and staring Dax down. "Fucking hell. Just what we need the night before the mating ritual. We've got wolves coming in from all three packs, hoping to find mates, and instead they're going to find god-damned demon dragons."

"You're lucky we were here. If you've got an infestation of demon dragons, you'll need our—" Dax glanced down at Steele, "—my help to hunt and destroy them. Unless you want a case of the Bubonic plague and everyone's vital organs MIA on your hands."

Oh, no. Fleur shook her head, not allowing the tears bubbling there to fall. Even Steele's friend had given up on him. Fleur couldn't. She wouldn't.

The biggest of the wounds she had under her hand seemed to be bleeding less. Olympus above, please don't let it be because his heart wasn't pumping.

Her fingers trembled as she placed two fingers on his neck. She was shaking too badly to feel anything. Either that or she would have to admit she couldn't feel his heartbeat.

"We wouldn't have this problem in the first place, if you two hadn't decided to do your dicking around in my town." Niko stepped up, chest to chest with Dax.

Fleur wanted to tell him to back off. Couldn't they see Steele needed help, not a pissing contest? Bastards.

But a mere human with a little bit of flower nymph heritage didn't simply tell the Alpha of the packs to step off. Not the night before the mating ritual where she hoped to find a mate.

Besides, yelling at the men wouldn't help Steele. If only she'd studied traditional western medicine instead of botany and herbalism.

"You were supposed to protect our women, not put them in jeopardy. I trusted you with their lives." Kosta pushed Heli behind him and got in Dax's face too.

May Zeus strike them down where they stood.

Dax didn't give them an inch. "We did, and my friend sacrificed his life to protect them."

That was it. She might lose her chance at going to the mating ritual, and she might piss off the Alpha, but she didn't give a flying squirrel if she did. Not if she could get some help for Steele.

"Shut the hell up, the lot of you. I'm trying to figure out how to save this dragon. Go measure your dicks somewhere else or help me."

Niko turned his glare on her, the rims of his eyes glowed with the wolf inside of him. Fleur glared right back.

He might be able to intimidate everyone else around him with that look and his inherent power, but just now, he could suck it. "Well?"

Zara sidled up to her mate and slid a hand into his. She spoke softly, soothing his beast. "Niko, quit trying to frighten Fleur. She's trying to save the hottie."

His wolf was close to the surface, in protection mode. But Zara had soothed this beast before. Fleur wasn't afraid. She understood he was trying to protect his pack, his mate.

Zara laid her head against Niko's chest. "The dragons did fight off a dozen of those beasts before we joined in. We only took out a couple."

"Fine." His voice wasn't so much a growl anymore. "Let's get him to Doc. Maybe he can help."

Yes. She should have thought of that. Doc was the pack's healer. Wolves didn't get sick, but he patched them up after battles.

Serena stepped into the circle that had formed around Fleur and Steele. "I already called him. He'll be here soon. But," she locked eyes with Fleur. "He's never worked on a dragon shifter before. I don't know that he'll be able to do anything."

TRIPPING TO THE AFTERLIFE

God dammit. He was dying.

No. no, no. Steele yelled the words, but they wouldn't come out of his mouth. Nothing in his body wanted to work.

He had to make it.

He would not leave Fleur. He had to protect her. Steele fought like hell to stay conscious, to hang on to life so he could be there for her.

Fleur, his beautiful, luscious flower. His true mate. He'd only met her hours ago, and he knew to his core they belonged together.

The beats of Steele's heart shuttered in his chest. Darkness pushed at the edges of his vison. The colors of the night faded to black and white. The only light left was the beautiful green of Fleur's eyes glowing from deep within. He held onto to that light, that love.

Even her eyes faded. He wanted to stay, needed to, for her.

The darkness overwhelmed Steele's consciousness, tunneling him under until there was nothing.

Steele died.

He felt himself slipping away while reaching for her with everything he had, but his soul. She already had that.

He'd left her alone in a world where demon dragons spread plague and death for shits and giggles. What an asshole he was to go and die on her. He should have been more careful, done more to protect her. He'd failed at the greatest duty a dragon had. Would she ever forgive him?

He did not understand how this had happened. One minute he had found his fated mate and the next he lost her. That was not how this story was supposed to go. Steele was a dragon warrior. No way he had lost a battle with a demon dragon.

His shard. The only thing he could think of was how he had lost all his power when one of the bastards had stolen his soul shard. He hadn't been wearing it when he first met Fleur, which was dumb. It gave him the ability to shift.

He would never understand now how he'd been defeated or how Fleur fared. Because he was dead and none of it mattered any longer.

Steele couldn't believe he was dead.

How was he even believing it? His thoughts still functioned but his body did not. That was too weird.

Voices filtered into his mind from somewhere far away. *"Why couldn't he stick to the fucking plan?"*

"Maybe because Steele didn't know about it, my love."

He heard a couple arguing and they were talking about him. Tally number two for the weird column.

Was it his parents? No. His mother had died almost a hundred years ago, but his father was still alive. A dragon well into his Wisdom.

Maybe this was the beginning of his life flashing before his eyes. Or perhaps the First Dragon was reviewing Steele's short one hundred and forty-four years of life to determine if he was worthy of the afterlife.

"What the hell are we supposed to do with him now?" A deep voice filled with the resonance of an alpha, a power like he'd never felt before rang through Steele's ears.

The voice had the ring of more than an alpha. Jakob's voice could command any green dragon to do his bidding. Match, the alpha of alphas had even more power. Neither compared to the pure power in this dragon's voice.

Holy alpha of all. He was hearing the voice of... the First Dragon. A flood of adrenaline tsunamied through him, prickling at every sense he had.

He was pulled from the total darkness into a shaded forest, where the trees grew taller than he'd ever seen, and the earth below was warm and fertile. This place was warm and comforting, like home. Again, he didn't really understand where he was or how he was there. He only knew he wanted to stay. Everything in him said this was the green dragon afterlife. Paradise.

Through a mist, a dragon with scales every color of the rainbow and a gash through one of his wings appeared, circling Steele, looking him up and down, growling between breaths, snorting smoke and wisps of flame.

He should have fought harder. Killed more demon dragons. Protected Fleur. His body didn't seem to exist, yet he had the feeling he was being measured and weighed.

"Well, aren't you a dumbass?" The voice boomed through the forest and shook Steele to his core. The sound had gone directly into his head and bored into his skull.

"Yes, I'm talking to you, dumbass. You fucked my plans right up by going and dying. Inanna practically served your true mate up on a platter for you and what do you do? You fucking die before you can claim her."

Steele didn't know how to respond to that. Sorry didn't quite cover it.

A woman, heart-wrenchingly beautiful, soft and warm, ghosted through the misty veil and clung to the dragon's front leg. "Don't be so hard on the boy. He found her, didn't he, all the way across the ocean. We didn't exactly make it easy. Poor youngling was so close to claiming her. He'd already gained his power."

She smiled at Steele and the adrenaline inside subsided. Her power wrapped him in the smell of fresh baked bread, a crackling fire, and love. Home. She was the very essence of this place.

"He didn't find her, your gift to her sucked him in. You practically placed a blinking neon I'm-your-mate sign above her head." The dragon snuffled the woman's hair and his fury subsided for the moment.

Or, less than a moment. He glared at Steele and snorted. *"He never should have taken the shard of his soul off. Then he could have claimed her right away. But, no. He left himself vulnerable, just like Jakob."*

The First Dragon pointed a talon at Steele. *"Those pieces of shit Galla Dragons almost stole his dragon-forsaken soul."*

The woman in white patted the dragon's cheek. "He is young. Younger than Jakob, and it was your idea to give them their powers before they claimed their mates."

That must be what had happened when Steele put his

shard back on after the party. Those powers had helped him destroy half a dozen demon dragons.

They hadn't helped him stay with Fleur.

The dragon flapped its wings in a way that Steele recognized was like throwing his hands in the air. *"They weren't supposed to wait. Powers, claim, mate, dragon babies, victory. Seems pretty damn clear to me. Being young is even more reason he shouldn't have died. He had another four or five hundred years. The dumbass. Do you know how many Galla Dragons he could have defeated in four centuries?"*

The woman in white grinned like she found his rampage at Steele cute. "Then you'll just have to send him back."

"How the hell am I supposed to do that? He's dead. D. E. A. D. Dead." The First Dragon paced in front of Steele, his scales rippling, sending showers of red, blue, gold, and green sparks through the air.

"Use the girl."

Girl? Steele glanced around but saw only more trees. Did she mean Fleur?

Steele knew Fleur was something special. More than the half of her that was flower nymph. But, he hadn't been able to tell what she was. He had scented something in her that cried out shifter, but it was so deep, he wasn't sure.

Maybe he was wrong. Could she be a necromancer? Those dark powers weren't right. Fleur was love and light.

The dragon shook his head. *"The flower? She's a witch. She can't have them."*

The woman in white countered him with a confident nod. "Let her use the gifts we bestowed upon her father, and his father before him, and his father before him."

There were legends told to every dragon warrior about

how the First Dragon's mate, the White Witch had given gifts, special powers to each of their children.

Steele received the gift of dragon's breath, a healing touch, from his father, who'd gotten it from his father, and so on up the line to the first green dragon son who'd been given the gift by his mother.

This woman, who felt like a mother to him, was…she was the mother of all dragons. The White Witch.

The shock and awe of that fact hit Steele right in the throat. He couldn't swallow, He could hardly breathe.

He guessed that didn't matter since he was dead.

"No, no, and nope. The flower is female, and those are dragon powers."

There was no such thing as female dragons.

The White Witch tsked at him. "Kur."

His name rang through Steele's head, digging deep into his psyche to find a place to hide.

"What?" He rolled his eyes exactly the way a recalcitrant youngling dragon who knew they were whining would.

The First Dragon and the White Witch had been dead for hundreds of years. Long before Steele had been born.

Dead. Like Steele was now.

Holy First Dragon.

It was them. The mother and father of all Dragonkind and he was standing here like a dumbass.

They were not what he expected. They were…almost normal, an old married couple you'd see in a sitcom. He liked them.

"My love, my mate." She took his fisted claws, uncurled them and kissed his palm. "You can't protect Ishtar by hiding her from the world any longer."

Who was Ishtar and why were they hiding her? What about Fleur?

"*I can, and I will.*" He spoke softly to her now. "*We're not talking about Ishtar, we're trying to figure out how to get the flower and this dumbass together.*"

She uncurled his other fist and gave that hand the same treatment. "Kur, sweetheart, it's always about Ishtar. She is our daughter. Our hope."

Whoa. No legend, no archives, no dragon had ever said anything about The First Dragon and the White Witch having a daughter.

The First Dragon closed his fists again, the tension rippling through the air around them. "*Which is why we have to protect her.*"

One by one, she pulled his talons open. "She will die if you don't allow her the freedom to fly. She's been cooped up for almost seven hundred years, and in all that time you haven't allowed a single dragon daughter to assume her powers. Sooner or later he will find out about Ishtar."

The First Dragon roared, his scales rippling in rainbows across his body, his scales shimmering with light and fire taking over.

The White Witch took the First Dragon's jaw in her hands and laid her cheek against his. She stroked his scales. "Enough, my love. The world will need her and all the dragon daughters to win the coming battle. Let the flower bloom, it will make both Ishtar and me happy."

The First Dragon huffed and puffed, pacing between the trees. Steele was all but forgotten. He gathered all the will he had to get their attention, to remind them about Fleur and whatever gift they were going to give her. Whether it helped him back to life or not, she needed whatever they had for her to survive against the demon dragon scum.

The White Witch and Steele watched the First Dragon growl and snort fire. He took to the air and circled the treetops.

Steele growled and reached for his own dragon self. He could feel the change inside of him pushing to get out, to protect Fleur even from the afterlife.

The First Dragon stared down at him from his angry flight.

"Calm yourself, dumbass. You will be back with your mate soon. If she's anything like mine, you'll need all the help you can get to protect her."

A moment later he landed and easily slipped into his human form. "You're damn sneaky, woman, giving me and my sons daughters. How can I say no to you?"

The White Witch blew a kiss to Steele, and did the same to her mate. "You can't. Besides, the gift was not entirely for you. And you love my sneaky side."

He chuckled. "Do I?"

"Yes, you do."

He proved her right by kissing her hard enough to make Steele squirm watching them.

She broke the kiss but stayed in his arms. "Now allow the flower access to her powers. She already feels them bubbling inside of her."

He stole another quick kiss from her. "Fine."

The First Dragon turned his full attention to Steele, baring down with his eyes, speaking straight into his soul. "Steele Greendragon, you dumbass. Listen to me and listen close.

Don't let those Galla Dragons steal your soul again. They don't know what the fuck to do with it anyway."

A ripple of power went through Steele. A fine green mist rose over and around, blurring his vision so they were only silhouettes. His voice rang in Steele's head still.

"You claim that flower and you give her your soul. She'll keep it safe. Don't dick around about it, either. Wake up. Claim her. Give her your soul. Protect her. Give her a good six or seven orgasms so she likes you—"

The White Witch smacked the First Dragon's side. Then she addressed Steele. Her light shone so brightly. Each of her words wrapped around him, imbuing him with a sense of love he'd never known existed. "She'll like you just fine, youngling, just make sure she feels the love you have in your soul for her."

Steele swallowed and nodded, soothed by her words and her love.

Then she winked at him. "Give her at least a dozen orgasm."

The First Dragon nodded. "I find the more the better to woo your mate." He pinched the White Witch's butt, and she squealed, but a lust beyond description sparked between them. The First Dragon pulled her tight to his side, kissing her neck, until she wriggled out of his hold and nodded to Steele. He thought for a second they were going to go at it right there.

"Right." He pointed at Steele. "It's time for you and your brothers to stop screwing around with these pansy-ass battles and defeat the Black Dragon and his offspring already. Enough is enough. You hear me?"

Steele's voice rose up for the first time, and he could speak again. "Yes, sir."

"If you die again, I'm going to kick your scrawny ass." He would do it too, from the afterlife or not.

"Yes, sir."

"Don't make me come down there."

Steele shook his head.

"No, sir."

"Good." He glanced into a distance Steele couldn't see and blew out the healing breath of a green dragon. It disappeared into the void behind.

"Oh, Kur, my love, this youngling probably doesn't need to remember anything about me or Ishtar and the others."

"He won't remember anything but what we told him to do. Will you, dumbass?"

Steele wanted to remember. He needed to tell the AllWyr council what he'd learned. "No, sir."

He looked far beyond Steele. "Alright, here she goes. One more thing, youngling."

"Yes, sir?"

He glanced at the White Witch and dipped his head, lowering his voice. She gave him a glare, but he chuckled and whispered to Steele anyway. "This will drive your mate insane, I promise. When you've got your head between those lush thighs of hers, use your dragon tongue to—"

Steele was pulled from the light of wherever he'd been and into darkness again.

DRAGON'S BREATH

A beat-up red pick-up truck screeched to a halt and its headlight fell out, clattering to the ground. A man who Fleur had always considered a silver fox jumped out with an old-fashioned doctor's bag under his arm.

Doc. That's all she knew of his name, just Doc. They'd had plenty of friendly conversations about her medicinal herbs and how either or both of them could help the pack. They were both outsiders who'd been taken in by the Troikas.

He gave the women and their wounds cursory glances but made it to Fleur's side within a few moments.

"What kind of shifter is he?" Doc asked looking Steele up and down with a frown.

"Dragon," Fleur answered.

Doc raised his eyebrows, but then nodded. "Okay, I got this. Move aside. Let me see what I can do."

Fleur gripped her pendant and Steele's crystal, and breathed a sigh, not exactly of relief, because Steele wasn't out of danger. Maybe the situation wasn't completely hopeless now.

With her breath, a green wisp flowed out of her mouth and drifted over Steele's body.

Whoa. She hadn't even eaten garlic or onions or anything.

Doc lifted his hands, not willing to touch this new unknown. He glanced at her and shined his pen light at her mouth. "What are you?"

She pulled her lips in and closed her mouth tight. Great, even the medically trained healer who dealt with shifters and witches and Zeus knew what other kind of beings on a daily basis thought she was a weirdo. But right now, who cared? If her unknown level of weirdness helped Steele, she'd take it.

The green breath swirled around Steele's body and seeped into him. It gathered at his chest and the light intensified.

Zara knelt beside her, glancing back and forth between Fleur, Doc, Niko, and the green swirls. "What did you do, Fleur?"

Zara grabbed her hand and squeezed.

Fleur welcomed the support her friend gave. "I don't know."

"It's dragon's breath." Dax's voice sounded awed. He stared at Fleur too, studying her.

She covered her mouth, the crystal dangling from her fingers. Okay, this was getting embarrassing. "I swear, I brushed my teeth."

The light swirls seeped into the wounds, closing them before everyone's eyes. The color that had been slowly fading from him shot back up his neck and face.

"Steele?" She reached out, touching his chest with her hand, pressing his crystal to his chest.

He sat straight up and sucked in a deep ragged breath,

gasping. Steele smacked his hand over hers and the crystal, holding both tight to his chest.

Both power and joy streamed through her body, sparking like a million lighting bugs. He was alive and so was she. Her senses were flying high. Little wildflowers popped up through the cracks in the sidewalk around them.

The tattoo of the dragon flickered across his skin, scales rippled up his neck and his eyes changed from dark round pupils to elongated with a deep green glow in his irises.

He looked at Fleur and growled. "Mate?"

Uh, no. His fist only tightened around hers. The heat flowing back and forth between them, where they touched, was scorching, but in a good way.

Dax grabbed Steele's shoulder. "Dude, I thought you were dead."

Steele took a long moment to drag his eyes from Fleur's and look at his friend. "I think I was. But, I needed to get back to my mate."

Both Fleur and Dax's mouths dropped open.

"Your mate?" Dax shook his head. "I doubt that dude, but you should at least make her your companion. She did save your life. Your girl has dragon's breath."

Fleur cringed at that. She was grateful Steele was alive, she just didn't believe she had anything to do with why. Dragon's breath didn't seem like a good thing, even if Dax thought that was what brought Steele back. Made her even more a freak than she was before.

Steele stared at her. Shock flashed through his eyes first, but it was quickly replaced by approval. He nodded and smiled at her, like he expected nothing else.

A warm glow she refused to identify took up residence

around her heart. A twitch started up behind her eye. Feeling like what she was having for Steele were reserved for mates.

He had called her his mate.

No. That had to be the adrenaline talking.

"I'd still like to take you to the clinic, young man, and check you out." Doc pointed to the pick-up truck.

Steele shook his head and got to his feet, pulling Fleur up with him. "I'm fine now, but thank you. A shift and some sleep and I'll be good as new."

"Steele." Fleur tried to pull her hand away. "I think you should go with Doc. You were…" It was hard to get the words out. She couldn't say dead. That word hurt too much. "Almost killed."

"Yes, my little flower, but you saved me. I'm here because of you."

Selena smiled, looking back and forth between Fleur and Steele. "Well, that's got to be the first case of resuscitation by bad breath."

Fleur did not like that look on Selena's face. It was entirely too match-makey. She wasn't supposed to want Fleur to be with anyone but a wolf from one of her son's packs.

Fleur wasn't supposed to be with anyone else. She was going to find a wolf at the mating ritual tomorrow. Simply because she's saved Steele did not mean anything. Nope. No. It didn't.

Zara stepped back and took Niko's hand. "Uh-oh. I recognize that look on your mother's face."

Niko chuckled. "The only ones who need to fear my mother are the unmated wolves coming to the ritual tomorrow night. And only then if they think they're leaving with their bachelorhood's intact."

Okay, phew. Fleur was on board with that.

Selena shook her head. "I do think we should talk to these new dragon friends of ours about being at that ritual tomorrow night."

"I don't want more trouble. Can you two guarantee the safety of our women?" Niko scowled.

Fleur had always been a little in awe of Niko. He was the ultimate alpha. Until she'd met Steele.

Now she was just confused. Because she wanted to slap the dirty look right off Niko's face. "There are no guarantees in life."

"I'm proof of that," Steele said. "What happened after I… "

Heli crossed her arms. "We kicked demon butt."

Jules giggled and nodded. "Fleur, girl, you might not be a shifter, but you've got some kickass powers at your disposal. That was some next level Wicked Witch of the West stuff you did with those trees. Maybe we should start calling you Elphaba."

Selena touched Fleur's free arm and gave her a little squeeze, grinning at her like she knew something Fleur didn't. "There seems to be more to our Fleur than any of us knew."

Yeah, including Fleur herself.

A COLD BATH FOR A HOT DRAGON

Steele was anything but fine. Physically, his body was recovering rapidly, thanks to his dragon and Fleur. He'd defeated death, and now he needed to protect and claim his mate. She was his. He knew that now, and he was shaken by the power of what that meant.

His true mate, a gift from the First Dragon and his mate, the White Witch.

He never expected to find her. His Wyvern, Jakob Zeleny had found his true mate recently and the entire dragon community had gone bat-shit bonkers over it.

Dragons had taken many human companions and lovers for centuries and those unions had produced thousands of dragon sons. No dragon warrior had found a true mate since the First Dragon had died seven-hundred years ago.

Until Jakob. Now Steele.

Jakob's power had increased to well beyond that of any other dragon alive, but his soul was now tied to another, making them both vulnerable in ways the entire dragon community was trying to sort out.

Steele had felt the surge in power, and the crippling vulnerability tonight. Now his soul, his dragon, and frankly his libido, were crying out to claim Fleur.

The sooner he could bite her, mark her, claim her and bed her, the better.

He still held her hand tight to his chest, along with his shining shard. He would give it to her, give her his soul, just as soon as he claimed her.

He wrapped the ends of the cord around her fingers. "Little flower, can you tie this around my neck again?"

"Yes, what is it? Why did the black lizard men want it?"

He released her hand just long enough for her to reach around his neck and knot the broken cord.

The dragon part of himself practically purred at having her arms around him. It pushed him to rub himself all over her. He would do that and so much more.

"They are demon dragons, and I don't know why they were trying to take it. But I'm glad you rescued it, because it is quite literally a piece of my soul."

She gasped and her eyes widened, the green looking deeper, richer than before. "Your soul? But how?"

He closed his eyes for a brief moment and inhaled her floral scented skin and hair. He could hardly wait to see how her pussy tasted. "I'll explain it all after we get you back inside. There could be more demon dragons lurking."

Niko butted in before Fleur could respond to him. "How many of those damned things are here?"

Steele didn't take his eyes off of Fleur. The moment his pendant hit his chest, it glowed and so did Fleur's necklace. Both with the same rich green.

She glanced down at her necklace, then at his shard. He

took her hand in his again. Both the shard and her hands imbued him with warmth and power.

Niko growled low in his chest. The wolf needed to protect his mate just as much as Steele needed to ensure Fleur's safety. He deserved an explanation.

"There are many more demon dragons than dragons in the world. Hell creates new ones faster than we can kill them. If they have come to Rogue because of us, I'm sorry for that. But we will stay and battle them as long as is needed to protect you, your mates, your children, and the souls of your clan."

"Fuck me." Niko's fangs and claws extended again. "They already killed you once, you asshole. How in the hell do we get rid of them?"

Steele pushed Fleur behind him, returning Niko's partial transformation with his own.

Dax butted in. "Steele and I have trained since childhood to fight against them. We'll teach you what we can, and call for reinforcements."

"You fucking do that. We just ended a war, I don't want to get involved in another one."

Enough. He'd given all the attention he was going to allow to anyone else. "We can discuss plans and strategy tomorrow. Now I need to take Fleur back up to her apartment and make sure she is unharmed and safe."

Niko growled deeper, but his mate held him back. Smart woman. Steele may have been defeated by the demon dragons for a moment, but now that he was back and had Fleur by his side, he was stronger and more powerful than before.

The wolf would be no match for him.

Fleur shook her head. "I'm fine. I'm not the one who died tonight."

Dax moved to their side, putting himself between them and the angry wolf alpha. "Yes, but you did do something no one who isn't a green dragon has done before."

"It must be…" Fleur broke off, she sucked in her cheeks and frowned. "I was going to say inherited from my mother, but that doesn't seem right."

Something niggled at the back of Steele's brain. He couldn't quite grasp it though. "What about your father? What was he?"

"Umm." Fleur looked around at the other people. She was hesitant to tell any of them. She shifted from one foot to the other and looked down at the ground. "I never knew my father, and my mother wilts if I even try to bring him up."

Selena clapped her hands three times to get everyone's attention. "Let's get everyone home now. Boys, you can each take one of the other ladies, can't you? The rest of the enforcers can escort the remaining women from the party and get them home safely. It's a big day tomorrow."

Fleur gave Selena a grateful glance, and Steele kicked himself for pushing her to reveal part of herself like that in front of all these people.

He'd make it up to her.

Selena came over and looked between him and Fleur, quirking her head to the side, then smiling. "Fleur, dear. Let your dragon take you back upstairs."

"But I—" She shook her head and again tried to yank her hand from his grip.

He was never letting her go. Never.

"I know you don't need him to, but it will make him feel better. He's had a long night, what with dying and all."

Fleur glared at him. The fire inside her made her so damn

adorable he wanted to lick every bit of her skin right there in front of everyone. He had a new idea to use his dragon tongue to —

"Fine, but you're helping me clean up."

He'd scrub her toilet if she asked him to, and he didn't even clean his own bathroom.

They all went back into Fleur's apartment. The she-wolves, their mates, and the enforcers gathered the rest of the women from the party and broke off into groups. Dax got nominated to escort two especially giggly ladies who'd decided to make more cocktails for all the non-shifters while they waited for the coast to clear. Steele recognized one of them as the crab-clawed pincher. He'd warn Dax, but the dude would probably enjoy it.

The three of them were the last ones out of Fleur's place. She shut the door behind them and leaned back against the wood, closed her eyes, and sighed.

Finally, he had her all to himself, and the first thing he was going to do was carry her to her shower and then her bed.

She still had his blood on her, and looked exhausted. That was mostly his fault.

His dragon tore at him to claim her, right the fuck now. But he held a tight rein, keeping the beast under the skin. He would care for her, make sure she felt the love that was in his soul for her first.

Love. Yes, so much more than pure lust. It blew his mind that he could be head over tail in love with a woman he'd met only a few hours ago, but he was.

It must be what knowing there was one person made especially for you, and you for them, meant. She was beautiful, and special, and talented, and all the things he could ever want in a mate. While all that had him completely attracted to her, his soul recognized her amazing inherent value, just being her.

"Okay, Steele. Everyone's gone, I'm safe, you can—whoa."

Steele picked her up under her legs and headed to where the bedroom and bathroom had to be.

She wrapped her arms around his neck, clinging to him like the side of a cliff. "What are you doing, we discussed this. I'm too heavy to be carried around like this, you'll drop me."

As if. "The only place I'm dropping you is on my cock, after you've had a long shower where I rub soap all over each and every one of your curves."

She stopped clinging and paddled her legs, wriggling in his arms. "Put me down right now."

What he wanted was her wriggling under him. "No."

"I will scream my head off bringing every wolf shifter in the city back here to tear you apart." She took in a deep breath, scrunched up her eyes and opened her mouth wide to do exactly as she'd declared.

Steele set her down, but he also pushed her back against the wall and covered her open mouth with his own. He licked and caressed her tongue with his, inhaling her flavor.

She resisted for the briefest of seconds, then she wrapped her hands into his hair and kissed him back with as much fervor as he was giving to her.

She broke the kiss with a bite to his lip and gave him a shove.

His dragon groaned, loving the rough side of her, the part that had given in and then continued the chase.

"No, means no, buster. Get that through your damn dragon head."

That was actual anger in her eyes. Gulp.

"I'm sorry." He searched for the right words to appease her. "Do you want me to ask permission each time I want to kiss you?"

His dragon was quite literally laughing at him in his head. But he would do whatever it took to be with his mate even if it was learning a new way to be in a relationship.

"What? No, eww. I don't want a guy who is submissive. I like the alpha bit. But even an alpha needs to make sure I'm actually on board for it first."

Okay, he could work with that. "Are you on board for a hot shower where I wash your body and eat your pussy?"

The tiniest of smiles quirked at the side of her mouth, and the sparkle in her eye said she liked that idea. A lot.

"Yes, but not now and not with you. I am going to the mating ritual tomorrow. I probably already smell like you as it is. I'll need about a thousand gallons of my homemade body wash to smell like me again."

Oh, hell no. He laid his hands on the wall on either side of her shoulders, caging her against the wall. She was his from now until eternity. No wolf, dragon, man, or any other male would ever, ever even sniff her. "You are not going to the mating ritual."

Her face did some eye and brow gymnastics. First her eyes went wide and her brows up, then she narrowed them into a glare, and finally she raised one eyebrow. God, it would be fun learning all her expressions. But the ones he most wanted to see right now were the ones she made when she came. On his cock.

She poked him in the chest three times, punctuating each of her words. "Yes. I am."

She didn't know. She wasn't a dragon. He didn't even

know what exactly she was, so maybe she didn't understand. He only barely understood this mating pull himself. "You are my mate."

She pinched the bridge of her nose between her thumb and forefinger and sighed. "Look, Steele. I will admit you're sexy as hell, and I'm more attracted to you than I want to be." Her gaze flicked from his eyes to his lips and back. "You kiss like Bacchus himself. Just because I saved your life doesn't mean we're mated. We have a connection, yes, but I'm mating a wolf. Tomorrow. It's my destiny."

Fuck a duck to hell and back.

Fleur skirted under and out of his arms and popped into the bathroom before he could grab her and kiss some sense into her. Instead he found himself thumping on the door. "Fleur, let me in."

"Go pound sand and not my bathroom door. If you break it, I'm sending you back to whatever afterlife you were in, because that's where my landlord will send me."

The water turned on, and an earthy soapy scent wafted under the door. Coconut, moss, something floral. The other thing he scented was her arousal.

She might be denying them both at the moment, but he was assured that at least her body was responding to him.

A faint buzzing sound came through the door. An electric razor? Not in the tub.

A vibrator?

If she started moaning he was going to break the door down and her landlord could bite him. Her orgasms were his to provide and he'd be damned if she ever needed to own a self-pleasuring toy ever again.

"Fleur, why don't you let me come in and do that for you?"

The buzzing stopped. "You can hear that?"

"Yes, baby, and it's killing me. You don't need that thing anymore. I promise my tongue will feel better."

She opened the door and pointed an electric toothbrush at him. He barely noticed it because she was wearing nothing but a towel, loosely wrapped around her, and it was slipping.

Her creamy bronze skin just begged to be uncovered and worshipped. Come on, towel, give a little more.

"I am not letting you brush my teeth with your tongue. Now, go home, or wherever you're staying." She waved the toothbrush around and with each movement of her arm, her towel came undone a little more.

If he could make her mad enough to really go at him, she'd be naked in no time.

She tried to slam the door on him again, but he smacked it with his hand, holding it open. "I'm staying right here, flower, and there's nothing you can do to stop me.

His voice came out lower and gruffer than he meant. But a new wave of her arousal shot between them like an avalanche.

"I'll take you to bed, and love you long and hard, and then soft and slow, over and over, until your mind and body are in such a state of bliss you'll never want me to leave."

Her neck and faced flushed and her eyes dilated. Yeah, she wanted that, too.

"You...you...," she swallowed and backed away, still waving the toothbrush like a sword. "You...dinosaur. You're going to ruin everything. I've got a destiny, dammit."

Destiny Schmestiny. He'd never thought fate had plans to give him a mate, yet here she stood.

"The only thing I'm going to ruin is your desire to mate a wolf." He pushed his way into the bathroom. The steam from the water running into a mountain of bubbles in the tub, wafted into her bedroom through a connecting door. He was no blue dragon, but if she wanted to have bathtub sex, he would oblige.

It wouldn't be as fun as rolling around in say, a forest, or a wide-open field, or the mud, but there would be plenty of time for that. Just as soon as he convinced her she was his mate and claimed her.

"Come here and take off your towel, let me see more of your luscious body." He continued forward and Fleur backed up with each advance. "Let me kiss and suckle each of your curves, let me fill my hands with your plump ass."

Her back was against the wall. He had her now.

"Did you just say my butt is big?"

Mmm. There was her fire.

"Yes, and I love it. I can hardly wait to bend you over so I can kiss it, and lick it, and fuck it."

A sound that was remarkably like a squeak came out of her mouth. She threw the toothbrush at his head.

He ducked, and she bolted past him and into her bedroom. He reached for her and snagged her towel, trying to grab her. All he caught was a glorious glimpse of all her nakedness before she slammed the door in his face. Again.

He'd be worried if he didn't hear her giggling on the other side of the door. Fleur was enjoying the chase as much as he was. The dragon part of him was practically jumping up and down clapping his hands. Only because he knew he'd catch her soon.

The other door to her room was in the hallway, and it was wide open.

Vines poked out from under and over the door, rapidly

growing across it and the ceiling. His shard glimmered and his dragon reveled in being surrounded by the greenery. Was Fleur doing this?

Within seconds the bathroom has turned into a full on green-house, with a complete mesh of vines covering the other door.

"Let's see you get out of that, dragon."

Steele approached the doorway, marveling at delicate weave blocking his way. He reached out to touch the plant, and a particularly large leaf smacked his hand away.

Unless Fleur was in imminent danger, there was no way he'd destroy her beautiful and creative attempt to escape him.

He knew he needed to claim her and soon, but morning was not that far away, and they both needed rest. He'd let her have the rest of the night to let the idea of being his mate settle in.

The water was still running in the bathtub. Now with the vines and leaves filling the room, the water seemed like a steamy spring. He could use a soak to soothe his muscles.

He turned off the water and dropped his clothes to the floor. When he climbed in he immediately wished Fleur was in there with him. One last try. "Your bath is nice and hot, little flower. Why don't you join me and let me wash your hair?"

He didn't say the hair on her head.

"Ha. Good try. Don't leave a ring of scales on the tub."

Damn.

The water only came up to the lower part of his chest, and his legs were long enough he had to bend them, but whatever she'd put in the water was fresh and earthy.

Every part of him relaxed, except his cock which had been hard pretty much since he'd seen Fleur the very first time.

He fisted it, wishing his hand was Fleur's instead. He had every intention of closing his eyes, imagining her hand, then her mouth on his cock. Within three long strokes, he'd fallen asleep.

Steele was flying through a pine forest. He was breathing hard and his lungs were working overtime. But not because he was tired. It was the excitement of the chase.

He caught a glimpse of the gorgeous pure white dragon as she weaved between a copse of trees a hundred yards ahead of him. She was a better flyer than he was, but he'd catch her.

Because she wanted to be caught.

She giggled and called to him, her sweet voice resonating in his head.

"Catch me if you can, mate."

"Oh, I'll do more than catch you, little flower."

He circled to her left and dove down, flying inches over the forest floor. His scales blended with the leaves and the ground cover, but he could spot her shimmering white body a mile away.

She zigged and zagged through the trees, slowing and looking over her shoulder for him. When she didn't see him, she circled back. Then he knew he had her.

She fluttered to the ground, landing silently, glancing around at the bushes, knowing he was hiding.

Her bright green eyes glowed so brightly, like the shard of his soul. It took his breath away.

Steele darted forward, folding his great wings in tight to push his speed. A half a foot in front of her, he swooped up landing on his feet in front of her.

She gasped and turned to run away.

Not this time. He encircled her with his wings, trapping her against him, embracing her.

"Now you are mine."

LEARNING TO FLY

*F*leur heard the water in the tub turn off and the splash of what must be Steele getting into her bath.

She let the breath she'd been holding go.

She wasn't sure how much longer she'd be able to hold out against his lascivious pursuit. Not because he would over power her, but because she wanted him something fierce.

The instant attraction she'd felt hours ago had only grown. The pure panic that swamped her when she'd thought he'd died was only part as strong as the overwhelming need she had to strip him naked and ride him like a happy cowgirl now that he was alive.

She didn't want to want him.

He was messing up her plans. Her destiny.

Aphrodite herself must have taught the man to kiss. Just imagine what that mouth could do between her legs. No mortal would be able to resist. She patted herself on the back for not begging him to take her on the kitchen floor the second everyone else had left.

The creeping ivy plant in her room was the only thing that had saved her from making a dragon-sized mistake. She'd focused all that sexual tension and frustration at the poor little plant and grown it into the cage of vines that were not only keeping Steele from getting to her, but keeping her from jumping his sexy ass bones.

Now he was naked on the other side of the door and she was ready to melt into a puddle of take-me-now right here on the carpet.

"Your bath is nice and hot, little flower. Why don't you join me and let me wash your hair?"

He didn't say the hair on her head. Whimper.

Be strong, Fleur. Don't let your dirty mind get the best of you.

"Ha. Good try. Don't leave a ring of scales on the tub," she called.

Silence. Was he finally giving up? She wasn't sure if she was relieved or disappointed. Both.

Another sound came from the bathroom. Holy hollyhock. He was moaning, and it was not in pain.

He was masturbating.

In her bathtub.

Without her.

Dammit.

And where was her god-damned vibrator? In the drawer under the sink in the bathroom. No use to her there.

If she got out of this alive, and by alive she meant with her sanity intact, she was buying a vibrator for every room in the apartment.

Fleur paced back and forth in front of the door, stopping to listen every few seconds. Was he groaning her name?

That hit her low in the belly and a wondrous tingle zipped between her legs.

Oh, Artemis help her.

She backed away from the door, and even though it was the middle of summer pulled out her long-sleeved flannel pajamas from the bottom drawer of her dresser. The green and white striped ones with teapots shaped like old English cottages all over them. She'd gotten them at a white elephant Christmas party. They were the unsexiest thing she owned.

She put them on, covering her nakedness and already feeling better. Yeah. Nobody would want to touch her in these ugly things. Not even herself.

She crawled into bed and pulled the covers all the way up to her chin. Stiff as a bored board, she laid there, straining to hear and then chastising herself for trying to listen to see if Steele was still getting it on in the bathtub.

She just needed to close her eyes and go to sleep. The evening had her completely exhausted, and morning wasn't even that far away.

The mating ritual was tomorrow, and she didn't want bags under her eyes and the yawns when her wolf mate-to-be came sniffing around.

The prospect wasn't half as exciting now, as it had been a few hours ago. Must be because she was so tired.

She tossed and turned, pressing her legs together to stave off the need that continued to grow.

Eventually she drifted off and began to dream.

Fleur was running through the forest, practically flying over the ground. An excitement she'd never felt before spurred her on and a giggle spilled out of her.

Sexual energy zinged through the air, playing with her

senses. The forest had a musky erotic smell, and even the wind tasted sweet, like whisky or wine. She must be at the mating ritual.

Yes, glowing eyes were chasing her. Her wolf's eyes.

"Catch me if you can, mate." This must be the wolf-link Zara and her other friends had told her about. Except didn't they use it when they were in wolf form. She wasn't a wolf.

"Oh, I'll do more than catch you, little flower."

She wanted him to catch her, but not too easily. That was half the fun.

He was behind her and closing in. She put on a burst of speed, but he didn't follow. Wait. Where did he go?

Fleur slowed and circled back. No way her wolf would lose her scent.

In an instant, he popped up in front of her. Sneaky bastard. His green eyes burned into her soul. She gasped and turned to run away.

Something big and strong, but soft and gentle, encircled her.

"Now you are mine," the wolf said.

She was. And he was hers.

But there was something wrong. Something that didn't quite feel right.

She turned back to her wolf and stared at him. His muzzle and furry ears were…ugly. This couldn't be her mate. The face she was looking at, the scent of him, even the feel of his body against hers were all wrong.

She didn't feel even the slightest bit of attraction to the wolf. Except there was a familiarity in his eyes. They were the only thing that felt true.

It was as if her mate was hiding behind a mask.

"Why are you hiding from me?"

The wolf growled, and it resonated deep in his chest, the sound vibrating so deep. "I'm right here, flower. But you don't want to see me."

She examined his face, trying to see through his façade. "I do. I've been waiting my whole life to see you, to know you, to be with you. But you're not you."

"You're only seeing what you think you're supposed to. Look closer, not just at me, but at yourself."

She frowned and glanced down at her chest and arms. Except her skin wasn't its usual tanned bronze and it wasn't her skin. She was white and was covered in scales.

Plus, her arms weren't even arms. Well, they were, but different, she had claws, or talons like a bird of prey, where her fingers should be.

Behind her, not only had her butt expanded, she had a fucking tail. And wings. She had giant white wings.

Her jaw dropped so far open, not only were the flies going to get in, so were the hummingbirds, Andean condors, pterodactyls, and jet airplanes.

Jesus, Mary, Zeus, and Hera. She was a dragon.

She glanced up, and a familiar green dragon, whose eyes matched his face now, stood before her, wrapping her in his wings.

He nuzzled her chin with his own, pushing her jaw back up and closed.

Suddenly, she was ultra-aware of everywhere his body touched hers. From his jaw, to his wings keeping her warm and safe, to the gentle, but exciting caress of his tail along hers.

"But I'm not a dragon. Am I?"

"I think this is just part of the dream. A vision from the White Witch."

As soon as he said that, a shimmer rippled across her skin and the scales faded into her own darker skin. Her hands and arms reappeared and so did her legs and butt.

What didn't reappear were her ugly pajamas.

She was still wrapped in Steele's dark wings, but now she was human and a stark naked one at that.

Steele's dragon tongue licked along his teeth like he was going to eat her up.

"What are you going to do to me?" She had a mouth again and the words hung between them in the air.

The same shimmer rippled across Steele's scales, and he shifted back into his human form. But his scales gathered and formed the tattoo on his shoulder and arm.

"I'm going to love you."

Just like that, her heart melted and the reticence she had for being with Steele burned away in the heat of his words.

She didn't know yet if she loved him, but she wanted to.

He laid her down onto a soft pile of leaves and grass, kissing and licking at her throat. "This is where I will mark you so the world can see you are mine."

She wanted him to bite her now, but somehow knew it wouldn't be the same here as it would in the real world.

He kissed his way down her body. "I doubt this will be the only time I'll dream about how magnificent your tits are."

His tongue circled one nipple, and his fingers played pinch-and-tease with the other. Each lick and nibble sent little bits of ecstasy coursing through her and pooling between her legs.

His mouth stayed glued to her chest, but his hand

wandered down, making lazy circles over her stomach, tickling across her belly button and then skating between her legs.

When his fingers met the wetness there, his head popped up, and he grinned at her.

"You've been wet for me all night, haven't you?"

Not the whole night. There was the hour before he arrived at the party, and the three minutes he'd been dead.

She shook her head.

"No use denying it, I can scent your arousal. Your need is hot and delicious, but earthy and natural, like a fresh picked Black Hungarian pepper."

She propped herself up on her elbows. "If you tell me you want to put me on a taco next, I'm out of here."

"I don't want to put you on a taco, but I do want to eat you."

Okay, she'd walked right into that one, and it was exactly where she wanted to be.

Steele skipped the kissing and licking his way to her pussy, and went straight down.

Oh, man. Her thighs were a jiggly mess and while he might say he liked her big ole butt, there was a whole lot there he hadn't seen yet.

"Your pussy is the most beautiful thing I've ever laid my eyes on. So ripe and pink, and wet. All mine."

Phew, he'd been distracted from her not so pretty bits by the magic of the vagina.

He wrapped one arm around her thigh, lifting her leg into the air. He licked from behind her knee, —who knew that felt so good—all the way to the widest part of her leg. "God, I love these thighs."

He nipped at the inside of one and then turned his head to

the other. "I want them wrapped around my waist at least a dozen times a day."

The tiniest smile broke across her lips. So, maybe her thighs weren't so bad.

"Put your hands in my hair, babe, and show me what you like." He lowered his lips to her clit and kissed it. Then didn't move.

He was waiting for her. She threaded her fingers into his hair, and he lowered his head, licking up one side, and down the other.

"Oh, yes." Her fingers instinctually gripped tighter.

Steele's tongue flicked across her clit once, twice, a third time, and then stopped.

"Don't stop." She pressed his head down, reaching her hips up to meet his mouth.

He hummed his approval and licked at her clit again. Over and over he lashed at her with his tongue, pushing her higher, her pussy throbbed and pulsed, needing his next taste.

She swiveled her hips, and his tongue swirled around, sending new waves of pleasure pulsing through her. Her other hand pushed into his hair, pulling it tight between her fingers.

"Steele, Gods, yes. Do that again. Please."

His hands bit into her thighs as he wrapped his arms around them. "Ride my face, baby, come in my mouth." He ground his mouth against her. His tongue was fucking magical.

She rocked her hips against his lips, her pulse beat out of control and her breaths were tiny gasps. "Yes, Steele, yes. Fuck, yes."

Her nipples beaded into hard nubs and her orgasm crashed over her. Her body jerked and spasmed, Steele pummeled her clit over and over with his tongue, drawing her orgasm out, until she could hardly breathe.

Her hands fell out of his hair, limply to her sides. He gave her one last long lick, sending another spasm through her core, and then crawled up her body.

"You are fucking sexy as hell, my little flower."

In her mind, she said "You're pretty damn sexy yourself." But what came out was "frnph frr nrr."

He chuckled and gave her a long kiss. She tasted herself on his lips, and that drove her to wanting to taste him.

Yeah, she wanted him badly. "It's your turn next. I swear. Just give me a minute to put my brain back in my head."

"Next time, love. If you're mouth goes anywhere near my cock right now, I won't last a second, and what I want more than that is to be so deep inside you that you forget any other man, or wolf, ever existed."

He settled himself between her thighs. She could feel the length of his cock, hard against her skin. He was so big, and she couldn't wait to feel him inside of her.

"Yes. Fuc—"

Tinga-ling-a-ling-ling. Tinga-ling-a-ling-ling.

Fleur rolled over and groaned into her pillow. Her alarm dinged at her, and if she had the four katrillion dollars it cost to replace her smartphone, she'd throw it against the wall and hope it smashed into teeny-tiny pieces.

She opened her eyes, blinking at the sun blaring into her room and found little daisies had sprouted up all over her bed.

Oh geez. How embarrassing. She quickly picked the flowers and put them into a leftover glass of water she had on her nightstand.

The smell of coffee, bacon, and some kind of carby deliciousness tickled her nose into wanting to go into the kitchen. But if she did that, she'd have to face Steele. Not the dream one. That was going to be real.

Real awkward.

HIS DAISIES

Steele whistled while he flipped the pumpkin pie pancakes. He was going to eat at least twenty, and then he was going to eat Fleur. He wasn't sure which would taste better.

Nah. He knew after last night.

Fleur. Definitely Fleur.

The oven dinged, and he pulled out the bacon. He loved that her kitchen was stocked with real food. Dragons, even green ones, could not live off rabbit food.

"Coffee?" Fleur stood in the doorway, rubbing her eyes, wearing the cutest ugly pajamas he'd ever seen. She had sex hair, no make-up, naked toes, and the most amazing blush to her cheeks.

If he wasn't already in love with her, he would have fallen hard right then. He was this close to picking her up and taking her back to bed again.

That hadn't worked out great last night. He'd ply her with his skills in the kitchen instead of the bedroom. For now.

"Hungry, babe?" He set the stack of pancakes on the table in front of her. She stared at them, then looked up at him.

"Coffee?"

She was probably still pretty damn worn out, and he didn't only mean from the battle with the dragon demons. He grabbed the coffee and mugs and poured her a hot cup.

She frowned at it.

Steele swallowed a chuckle. His little flower was not a morning person. There had been a big jug of Southern pecan almond milk creamer in her fridge, and as soon as he grabbed it and poured a couple splashes in, she wrapped her hands around mug.

"Mmm. Coffee."

"Such a sexy sleepyhead you are."

She took a couple sips before she answered. "Long night. Crazy dreams."

Oh, he knew all about her dreams. "What did you dream about?"

Fleur's cheeks went even more flushed and a little daisy popped up in the middle of the table, growing into a full-grown bloom in an instant.

"Nothing." Her voice came out as the tiniest of squeaks. She snagged the flower and shoved it between her legs under the table.

Steele pretended to pout. More so because he was envious of that daisy. He ought to be the one between her legs. "Aww, babe. You're going to hurt my feelings. Your screaming orgasm didn't seem like nothing to me."

Three more daisies sprouted around her chair. She stood up, sloshing her coffee on the table. "Were you eavesdropping on me while I was sleeping? That's just weird."

Steele picked up a piece of bacon and bit into it, watching her get all riled up. It was a bluff of course, she wasn't mad. A little embarrassed maybe, but what he mainly scented was her arousal and the sting of sexual frustration. He could fix that if she'd let him.

Maybe she would once they cleared just one thing up.

He stood and walked around the table. Fleur stood there, stiff as a tree trunk. He circled her, skimming the backs of his knuckles down her arm, to her waist, and then over her hip. Her lips parted as her breathing ratcheted up.

He walked behind her and slid his hand across the small of her back, to the dip at her waist, and then cupped her body to his. Fleur turned her head, unintentionally exposing the other side of her neck to him.

He bent his head, wanting so badly to kiss her neck, to suck on it, to bite her and make her his. Instead he pressed his lips to her ear. "I didn't have to eavesdrop, my love. I was there."

She gasped and three more flowers sprung from the floor.

"I was the one who made you scream. My mouth on your clit. Your hands in my hair, showing me just how you like my tongue to fuck your sweet hot pussy."

The flowers were popping up in bunches around their feet now. "Meep."

"You're right, it was a dream, and your poor little body hasn't gotten the satisfaction it's craving. I can scent how hot and needy you are for me right now. I'm fucking titanium hard, aching to get inside of you."

Fleur laid her head back against his chest, and groaned. "Steele."

She was so fucking hot. "Yes, baby."

"You're hard as steel."

He ground his cock against her backside, reveling in both the feeling of her body and the moan coming from her throat. "Yes, I am, and I'm going to stay that way until you let me take you to bed, to claim you."

"But the mating ritual."

He'd be worried, but her words had no oomph.

"We cleared that up last night. You'll never belong to any wolf. You are mine, and I am yours."

She sighed into his chest. "It was only a dream."

"Then let me make it a reality."

A daisy grew and encircled his leg.

"I…I want to. But what if that's not what is supposed to happen? The one thing my mother told me was that my destiny was here in Rogue. You're not from here."

"I'm here now."

"Why are you here?"

"I'm on R&R. This is a town full of shifters. Seemed like a good place to hang out and have some fun." But maybe something else had attracted him to Rogue. Something much more important.

Fleur nodded, and he could practically see the thoughts burning through her mind. "You don't plan on staying, do you?"

He'd never even considered it. He had a job to do. The demon dragon population in Europe was growing, and he had to keep the people in his area safe. "You'll love the Czech countryside, where I live."

She pushed against him and stepped out of his arms. He let her go, because this was not part of the chase. She truly wasn't sure she wanted to be with him.

"Steele, this place, the people who live here, are the closest I've ever had to a family. They accept me, and don't think I'm strange. I don't want to leave. The mating ritual gives me the chance to truly become part of their family."

A growl rumbled through Steele's chest. He was her destiny, her family, not some damn wolves. What did he need to do to prove that to her? "Look around. Even your powers are reveling in being with me."

"They've never been like this before." She reached a hand out toward a basket of herbs. The small plant doubled in size, filling the air with the fragrance of spices. "I can't deny it reacts to you."

"Because we belong together. You must see that, feel it." His own soul was on fire for her, pushed by his dragon to claim her now, make her understand there would be no one else.

Fleur placed a hand on his cheek, quieting the animal inside with her touch. But she incited it again with her words. "I do, but it doesn't mean I'm not confused. I still want to go tonight. I need to see what happens."

Fuck. He could lock her up, or better yet, fly her far far away, then lock her up with the rest of his treasure.

His gut clenched at the thought. His little flower needed sunshine and freedom to thrive. He would have to come up with a different way to convince her they were meant for each other.

He knew what to do. His dragon thrashed and writhed inside of him at the thought. It would never let her go. He had to trust that he wouldn't have to.

"I'll make you this deal. Go to your mating ritual tonight. Tempt every wolf there with your body, your beauty, inside and out. But understand I will be waiting. Because I know with every part of my being, my soul, that you are mine. Forever."

Fleur swallowed and stepped further away from him. The green of her eyes glowed along with her necklace. Steele knew without looking his own shard returned the light.

Before either of them could say anything more, Fleur's phone beeped with an incoming text. She grabbed it and flicked her thumb across the screen.

Steele saw the relief on her face, scented it from her, at having something else to do. But the relief turned to the acrid smell of worry and fear.

"What is it?"

His own phone dinged with a message from Dax.

"We have to go to the Sleepy Folk. Zara says there's trouble, and they need you."

"Yeah, Dax sent me the same thing."

"I'll go get dressed and drive you over there."

He nodded and let her escape the kitchen without agreeing to his deal. He would hold her to it regardless. One night. That was all he would give her. Anything more, and he would lose the battle with his dragon. He wanted to give her the time she asked for to appease her mind. It still blew his own that in one night he could go from being sure he had a lifetime of nothing but meaningless sex to having a true mate.

It was only fair he give her some time, too. The threat of the demon dragons meant he couldn't give her more than tonight.

He would risk her wrath over losing her.

They were silent on the way across town. They hadn't said

so much as another word when they walked into Kosta's Speakeasy.

It was closed for the day because of the mating ritual, so while the wolves met in the office, the girls pulled Fleur away to a booth in the corner.

Steele watched her go, wanting to kiss her again, make sure everyone here knew she was his. Instead he joined Dax over at the bar.

"I could use a fucking drink." Dax jumped over the bar and searched through the bottles.

Steele doubted the wolves had anything strong enough. "I think I talked to the First Dragon last night."

"Are you shitting me?"

"No." The shock and awe of everything that happened had him shaken. But at the same time, he felt a new sense of power and purpose.

Dax set two whiskey glasses on the bar and pulled a flask out of his back pocket. He poured two fingers of the red and amber liquor into each glass.

"This calls for some Dragon Spirit." Dax blew a puff of fire, lighting each of the drinks up. "What did he say?"

Steele stared at the glass and frowned. His memory was foggy but a few things he remembered. "He called me a dumbass for dying."

"Uh, that's weird. I mean, that was a pretty dumbass thing to do, but does the First Dragon even know words like that? He died in the 1300's. Didn't he call you like a crooked-nosed knave or something? That's what my dad always called me."

"Maybe that's just the way my mind translated it." He took a swig from the bottle. "The White Witch was there too. At least, I think that's who she was."

"Holy shit. What did she say?"

"I don't think she ever spoke directly to me. She spent most of the time chastising the First Dragon. They argued. A lot. I can't really remember it all very well."

It was like a dream, fading already the second he woke up. He had the feeling they'd laid some pretty heavy truths on him, but he couldn't grasp them in his memory.

Dax shook his head like he couldn't believe a word coming out of Steele's mouth. Steele could hardly believe it himself. Dax poured them both a second drink. "She argued with the First Dragon?"

Steele down it too, wishing another green dragon was here to put a little healing dragon's breath into the drinks. "Yeah, like an old married couple."

Dax shivered. "I'm so uncomfortable with this entire conversation."

"He also gave me sex advice."

"Dude, stop." Dax lit up another round of liquor. "He's our great-great-great-great and so on and so forth grandfather. He should not be giving anyone sex advice. Not to mention the fact you were both dead at the time."

The First Dragon and his mate, Ina, I-, crap he couldn't remember. They hadn't seemed dead. Especially when he'd been giving Steele instructions. Wake up. Claim. Protect. Orgasm.

Or something like that.

Wake-up and protect were as far as he'd gotten. Fleur wouldn't let him come even close to claiming her.

"Alright, dickheads, I mean dragons. What the fuck is going on, and if we kill you, will it go away?" Niko swaggered out of the office, flanked by his two less than happy looking wolf-shifter A-team.

All three of their faces were barely human, more wolf. Their eyes glowed silver around the edges. They were in protection mode, and Steele completely understood.

He stood and balled his fists at his side. Fighting with the wolves would not help him win Fleur. But it would make three less of them to be sniffing around her.

It also would not help him defeat the demon dragons, but kicking their asses would feel pretty damn good.

"If you kill us, you'll have a shitload of demon dragons in your backyard. I don't think you want their death and destruction *wyrming* its way into your mating ritual."

Dax poured each of the wolves a shot of their own whiskey and breathed just enough fire to set them all alight. "I've already contacted Match, the red Wyvern. He's making arrangements to fly here in time for the ceremony tonight."

If the red Wyvern himself were coming the situation was grimmer than Steele had first thought. His next call had better be to his own Wyvern, Jakob.

"We need less dragons, not more."

"Unless you want less wolves, you need more Dragons." As Dax spoke his voice got lower and darker. "The demon dragons are the purest evil in the world, and now that they are here, they'd like nothing more than to murder each and every one of your mates and spread a plague throughout your town."

The fire in each of the little cups grew from a tiny flame to a full on blaze, reacting to the heat coming off Dax.

Steele put his hand on Dax's shoulder, bringing his friend back from the darkness in the soul of every red dragon.

"Well shit," Max said, "Mom will kill us if we let anything happen to screw up this mating ritual. Just ask them to help us, Niko."

Niko snarled at his brother, then sighed. "What we should do is cancel the whole thing."

Max folded his arms. "You know Gal and I are ready to have the whole thing upstate if we need to."

"We can't." Niko shook his head. "Jules pulled one of her eyes roll back in her head and spoke in tongued thing. She told Zara it has to be here and now."

The flames in the drinks fizzled for a second at Jules's name. Dax had a look of more than interest on his face. Redheads were his thing.

Kosta sat on a stool and stared at the flaming shots. "Yeah, we have to do it. Mom isn't the only one who wants this to go well. Heli has already threatened to build me a doghouse in the backyard if I cancel." He pointed at Steele and Dax before downing his shot. "You assholes can figure out the fucking logistics of getting enforcers from three packs to work together."

"We will not let anything happen to anyone's mates. This I promise."

The future of his own mate depended on this damn mating ritual, so he'd do everything in his power to make sure it went off like a fucking birthday party if he had to.

At the end of the night, he and Fleur would be the one's celebrating.

SCENT OF A DRAGON

Fleur was a hundred percent going insane. How could she be so damn sure she was destined to be a wolf mate and have absolutely no desire to be with one in the slightest?

Because that stupid dragon had gotten into her head, and had come pretty dang close to getting in her pants, too. That was all she could think about.

He was so sure she was his mate.

No way.

Maybe.

Damn it.

"Fleur, dear. You seem a bit distracted. Can we help?" Thank goodness for Selena and the other Troika women.

"Not unless you know where I can get some dragon repellant."

"I wouldn't repel anyone that hot," Jules said. Zara slapped her on the arm and Jules shrugged. "What?"

"You're standing at a mating ritual about to find a wolf to mate. Remember?"

"Sure, sure." Jules waved her hand shooing Zara's concern off like a fly. "But if I wasn't. Mmm-mmm."

"Why are you avoiding him?" Heli asked.

Seriously? Fleur almost rolled her eyes. Heli had been with Kosta longer than any of the rest of them had been mated. She didn't even remember what it was like to be single in this town of hot wolf shifters. "The mating ritual is tonight. I don't want to show up smelling like a dragon."

"Uh, I don't think you can help that." Zara guffawed, but when she glanced at Fleur's face, she turned contrite. "Sorry. But it seemed like you two had more than a connection."

Fleur almost sniffed herself but held that impulse back. "Yeah, there's something there, but I don't know if he's the one I'm meant to be with. I just have this feeling that something is going to happen tonight."

Heli grinned at her. "How could it not? Wolves are coming from all our packs. A lot of somethings are going to happen."

"I know I'm not a wolf, but I appreciate that you invited me to come."

"Since the Troika alphas all mated the three of us a lot of wolves are interested in meeting humans and…," Zara motioned toward Fleur.

"Whatever I am," Fleur supplied. It was okay. She'd lived with knowing only a part of herself for long enough that she'd accepted that nobody else understood who or what she was either.

"Right. Whatever badassness you are, to see if their true mates might not be wolves. So, of course we invited you."

"We just want to make sure you still want to come." Galyna's voice was gentle and sincere.

"I do." She had to know for herself.

Selena searched her eyes and smiled. "Okay, then. While the guys are having their freak out over the security, I declare a spa day to remove the *l'eau de* Dragon from you. Besides, I could really use a massage from the sexy new masseuse I happen to notice started working at the Rogue Spa last week."

"Saleeeeeenaaaah." The girls all pouted.

"Fine, one of you girls can have him this time. I'll make sure to request him for my next one. I bought one of those massage subscriptions."

Heli rolled her eyes.

"I'll get Kosta to make the arrangements to have several enforcers accompany us, or we'll never hear the end of it. I suggest each of you go give your mate's a quick kiss and snuggle and reassure them, too."

The girls each went to find their mates and seeing the clear connections and affection between the pairs, a deep longing burned inside Fleur's chest and stomach. She glanced over at Steele and felt a sad hollow open inside of her. Was she wrong to want to go through with the mating ritual?

She slid out of the booth and walked over to Steele. This was probably a bigger mistake than wanting to go to the ceremony.

She wanted to reach out to him, touch him, feel that zing of energy between them. Instead of doing that she stared at her sneakers.

"Hi."

"Hello, little flower." He twisted on his barstool and pulled her between his legs. "Come to give me a kiss before you leave, too?"

Oh, yeah. There was the zing. "Yes, I mean, no. I mean, gah.

I don't know. I thought I'd at least tell you we were going so, you know, you didn't worry."

Geez, awkward much? She hated feeling this way. Like one dream orgasm had turned her into a bumbling mess of geeky teenaged hormones. Blech. She needed to get over that right away. How to do that was another matter.

"I will anyway, so you should give me that kiss. It seems to be helping the other men." Steele wagged one eyebrow indicating toward the couples around them engaged in various lip-locks.

"That's probably not a very good idea." She knew it wasn't because of how badly she wanted to do it. "In fact, I can't think of anything worse we could do."

"I've got a few ideas." He wrapped his arms around her, pulling her impossibly closer.

So close, in fact, she could feel something hard pressing against her stomach, and it wasn't a pencil in his pocket, but it might be a rocket in his pocket.

"You do, huh?"

"Yep. For starters, we could do this." He licked the shell of her ear.

"Oh, yeah, that's not good at all."

"And then we could do this." He nibbled his way down from the sensitive spot behind her ear to her collarbone.

"Definitely a horrible idea."

"After that we should—"

"Ah ahem." Dax leaned on the other side of the bar with his chin in his hands. "While I'm all in for watching you two go at it right here on the bar, you might have to wait to put on your show until later. The enforcers are here for their how-to-kick-demon-dragon-ass training."

Fleur blinked her eyes bringing herself back from the lustful fog her body had wrapped around her brain. Her friends were gathered in the doorway, and several of them were unsuccessfully stifling snickers.

What in Hades was she doing? She smacked Steele on the shoulder. "I told you it was a bad idea."

He chuckled, but let her go when she wriggled to get away.

By the time she made it to the group of girls, they were no longer holding in their giggle fits. Zara pretended to sniff her. "Getting one last dose of dragon before the spa?"

"Har har." So what if she was? It was a good dose too, that would have to last her for a very long time. Because after tonight, she wouldn't be getting anymore of him.

Now that sounded like a horrible idea.

"You're going to need a good two-hour soak in a mudbath to get that dragon's scent off of you."

She took the girl's good-natured ribbing in stride. It was either that or break down and tell them all that she was having second thoughts about the mating ritual. No way could she reject their offer, so kindly given. Even worse, she'd be rejecting becoming a part of their family. That was more important. Being a part of something bigger than herself would fill the void in her heart and soul.

"Well, then. Here's mud in your eye."

Her friends all laughed at her self-deprecating humor. All except Selena.

A few hours later, she was scrubbed, polished, and buffed within an inch of her sanity. She'd insisted on only all-natural beauty products and had even struck a deal with the spa's owner to provide them with a line of her own cleansing oils scented only with herbs and spices instead of all those harsh chemicals they'd tried to apply to her.

She might not want to smell like her dragon, but she also didn't want to repel every shifter this side of the Mississippi.

Wait. Her dragon?

No. That wasn't what she meant.

Whatever. This was not the time to think about that. The mating ritual was about to begin, and she didn't see Steele anywhere.

Not that she was looking for him. Better if he wasn't around.

Fleur stood with a group of the women who had been at the pre-mating party at her apartment. Most seemed carefree and relaxed, excited even.

Not her.

What if none of the wolves wanted her? What if none of them even liked her or wouldn't consider mating with her?

She opened and closed her fists trying to release this bout of negativity and anxiety that had grabbed a hold of her ever since she'd gotten to the forest.

It was nerves. That was all.

Everything would be fine.

People in the crowd started to hush, like they knew it was time to start. Fleur looked one last time around the groups for Steele. No, he wouldn't be here. He'd be in the woods, watching, protecting.

Selena walked to the center of the ceremony field, and the gathering went silent. Kosta, Max, and Niko all joined her. Niko spoke, the alpha in his voice ringing out through the night. "Tonight, we bring our three packs together. Through this mating ritual our people will bond, alliances will be made, and we will heal from the wounds of the past. We call upon each of the packs, bring forth the first of your clan to join the mating ritual."

Selena stepped up. "Rogue, who from our pack joins the mating ritual?"

"We do." One of the she-wolves from the party stepped into the circle, then another, and another.

"We do." Three young men joined the women in the circle.

"Serenity Bay, who from your pack joins the mating ritual?

"I do." A young man, but strong of build stepped into the circle and glanced at one of the Troika she-wolves. Looked like that alliance might already be formed.

"We do." Another small group of people joined the others.

A new energy charged through the forest. The mood was no longer somber, but an air of excitement pushed against them all.

"Grimm Falls?"

Two more groups of men and another band of women stepped forward.

"Welcome to you all. We wish you well in your search for your mates. Any others who wish to be mated, go forth, greet each other in the ways of our people, and should you find your true mate, may you live happily ever after."

Whoops and hollers rose up through the air about half the group shifted into wolves who all began circling and scenting each other.

The remaining group of humans in the circle, mostly women, were all approached by shifters who circled and sniffed them. Some giggled, one girl was toppled over by a large blonde man who shifted into his wolf and began licking her face.

Fleur waited and hoped. One wolf stepped tentatively near her, then turned quickly and trotted away. Uh, that was weird. Guess he wasn't the one.

When two more approached her and did pretty much the same maneuver, she wondered if the spa had snuck a strong-smelling lotion or perfume on her that she hadn't noticed. Shifter's sense of smell was sensitive and anything fake or artificial grossed them out.

She surreptitiously turned her head to sniff one arm and then the other.

That's when she noticed the big-ass green dragon standing a few feet from her in the trees. His scales blended in perfectly with the foliage around him and she might not have seen him at all except for the light beaming from her necklace. It seemed to do that a lot around him.

"You smell delicious, little flower."

The way he spoke into her mind reminded her too much of the dream she'd had with him. That was the last thing she needed to be thinking of on mating ritual night. "Go away, you're scaring off the wolves."

He chuckled right into her head. *"I know."*

Fleur crossed her arms doing her best to close herself off from him. "Dammit, Steele. I'm never going to get mated if you don't back off."

"You already have a mate." This time his tone was anything but jovial.

What if she didn't want one? Oh, who was she kidding? She did want a mate and a family. She knew in the first minute of the mating ritual none of the wolves were going to pick her. Actually, she knew this morning when she'd woken up with daisies sprouting all over her room.

So why was she fighting it so hard?

Stupid destiny.

Maybe destiny could go fuck itself.

"You said we had deal. You told me to come to the mating ritual and see if a wolf wanted me."

"I told you to come to the ceremony. I never said I'd let a wolf get anywhere near you."

"That's not fair." Yeah, cause life thus far had been fair. Where was fair when she'd grown up without a father and an absentee mother? Where was fair when every relationship she'd tried to have had fallen apart when they figured out she wasn't normal? And where the hell was fair when destiny decided to dick her around, let her think she'd found a family with the Troika's and then mated her to a god-damned dragon?

"All's fair in love and war. Especially when the battle is to win the love of my fair lady."

Screw destiny and screw Steele, and not in the fun way. "You're an ass. I'm going home."

Fleur stomped off, but Steele followed her. "Go away. I'm mad at you." More like mad at the world.

"I can't leave you in these woods alone. A dozen other dragon warriors are watching and waiting for the demon dragons to appear and wreak their havoc."

She might be miffed that a wolf wasn't going to make her part of the family. But those were still her friends out there. This night meant a lot to them. "Steele. You can't let anything happen to the wolves or their mating."

"Don't worry, my love. If the demon dragons do appear, our warriors will take care of them. The wolves will never know. We will ensure their lovemaking goes as planned."

"Lovemaking?" She guessed they were, but that wasn't how she'd thought of this night. In her head, it was family making.

"What do you think is going on all over these woods right now, sweetness?"

Two wolves ran by them, dancing around each other, nipping and dashing about, their animal sides flirting.

She didn't want to see this. Sure, she was happy for everyone who was finding their mates. But she could be just as happy for them at home with a pint of pistachio ice cream, too. Her car wasn't parked too far away. She'd be home watching re-runs of *Gray's Anatomy*, which was the perfect excuse to cry, in no time.

"Fleur. Wait." Steele loomed in front of her and before she could dodge him he'd wrapped his wings around her, the same as he'd done in her dream.

She tipped her head forward and rested it against his big chest. Inside this cocoon he'd made for them she could feel safe and secure. Instead she was crying.

Damn. Damn. Damn.

"I understood your anger, but the scent of sadness rolling over you now is breaking my heart."

She blinked quickly, trying to hold back the tears before Steele noticed. Too late.

His dragon tongue gently touched her cheek, wiping away the streaks.

"Is it really so bad to be my true mate?"

She swallowed back the rest of the tears. "No. It's just that, I thought I'd figured it all out."

"Figured what out?"

The wings around her became arms, and instead of scales her cheek lay against a warm human chest.

"Where my life was going. What I was supposed to do. I thought if I mated to a wolf, I'd finally…"

She was stupid. So, so stupid.

"Finally have a family, someone who loves you unconditionally, forever?"

Fleur jerked her head up and saw so much sincerity and vulnerability on Steele's face it took her breath away.

How did he know?

"I never thought I'd be blessed with a true mate. That just isn't the way of dragon warriors anymore. We fight, we hold back the evil in the world, we protect the innocent. But what is it all for?" He shook his head and the sad far away glint to his eye hurt her heart.

Steele brought one hand up and brushed a strand of hair from her face. She leaned in to his touch; she couldn't help it.

"I didn't know until you. You're the reason I am a warrior against the dark, and what I will continue to fight for the rest of my life."

"Steel, I—" She'd never been anyone's reason for anything. Did he really feel so deeply for her after only one day? She knew there was something inside of her that called for him to open her heart, to let him in.

She'd pushed it down, ignored it, even denied it, assuming it was wrong. Warmth grew in her chest and spread across her body, pooling in sensual swirls low in her belly. Could this dragon really be both her destiny and her soulmate?

She'd counted on having one, hoping for the other, but ready to settle for less.

"If you don't feel the same about me, I will do everything I can to be the man you want, that you need. If I have to woo you, court you, wine and dine you to make you fall in love with me, I will. Because I'm never giving you up, Fleur."

Maybe she didn't have to settle. For once, it felt like destiny was on her side.

Fleur touched Steele's cheek and brushed her lips across his. The grief she'd felt for the life she thought she'd lost with the wolves faded as the heat between her and her dragon built.

Yes, he was her dragon.

She wanted to yell it from the treetops, but her mouth and tongue were a little pre-occupied tasting and touching Steele's right now.

"I want you, Steele."

A rumble of pleasure resonated through his chest. "You can have me, babe."

He stripped his shirt up over his head revealing the rippling muscles she'd been crying on only a few minutes before. Sweet Aphrodite, he was hot.

His stomach didn't qualify as a six-pack, it was more like a twenty-four pack. She was going to lick every single one of them, too.

She was back in his arms before she could decide whether she wanted to start in on his full-case of abs from the top or the bottom. They sank down together to the forest floor.

Steele's hands were already up under the skirt of the filmy dress she'd worn tonight, and his lips were permanently attached to her neck. She didn't want them anywhere else. Except maybe her breasts.

She pushed him away long enough to slip the dress over her head. She was wearing a bold floral print matching set of bra and panties underneath.

"I love this look, but I'll love it even more when you're not wearing anything at all."

"Then you'd better take them off me." Her tone was more flirtatious with just a touch of sexy bedroom huskiness. She liked it.

"With pleasure."

He grabbed the strap over her shoulder with his teeth and slid it down her arm while unbuckling the hooks in back. Before she could say sixty-dollar lingerie, gentle cycle only, he'd tossed the bra over his shoulder and into the dirt.

She cared only for the point two seconds it took him to fill his hands with her breasts. "I'm generally an ass man, but these gorgeous tits might convert me."

He licked across the top of one of her breasts, dipped his tongue into her cleavage, and then across the other one.

"Yes, look how they overflow in my hands. Fucking gorgeous." He lowered his head again, this time taking a nipple into his mouth and sucking hard. A flock of pleasure crashed into her and fluttered its way straight to her clit.

"Ooh. Keep doing that."

"But the other one will get jealous." He switched from one breast to the other, playing with one nipple in his mouth and the other with his fingers.

"Someday I'm going to make you come just by sucking on your nipples, but that will have to wait. I've got too many other places to taste on you tonight. Lie back. Let's get these panties off."

She leaned onto her elbow and lifted her rear as he slid the stretchy lace over her hips and thighs. The panties went the way of the bra.

"Ouch. Rock in my butt." She reached around underneath

her, until she found the boulder poking her bum and tossed it aside. She didn't want anything to be uncomfortable for the serious sexy times she was about to have with Steele.

With a wave of her hand, the softest carpet of grass and wildflowers filled in the ground below them. She laid back in the grass and crooked her finger at him.

"Fuck, that's hot, Fleur. I'd roll around in the grass with you all night.

Fleur was totally down for that. She reached for his pants and opened them up, pulling out his cock. It was already so hard. She stroked him in her fist. "I want you inside of me, Steele. But this doesn't mean I wouldn't still like some wining and dining."

"I'll wine and dine you as much as you want. I'll spend the rest of our lives making you fall in love with me. First, I'm going to claim you and fuck you until we both forget our names."

A whole circle of daisies, fifty or more, sprouted up around them, fully grown, reaching their sweet petals inward as if waiting and watching the fun to come.

FINALLY MINE

Not one more minute, not another second. Steele would not wait any longer to claim his true mate.

His heart nearly beat out of his chest and flew into the sky to declare to all that Fleur had agreed to be his.

He would still have to work to win her trust, her love, to be allowed into the soft vulnerable part of her soul, but he would do it. He would do everything for Fleur.

The first thing he'd do for her was mark her and claim her, putting her under his protection forever more. Then they'd celebrate with a few rolls in the hay, or grass and leaves, as the case may be.

To mark Fleur, he'd have to draw his mouth away from her tasty tits and his lips were protesting that idea. They were thoroughly enjoying being attached to her soft rosy nipples.

Just one more taste and he'd work his way up her silky skin to her neck. He flicked his tongue over the hard bud.

"Ooh, yes." Fleur's hands pushed into his hair, keeping him in place.

He loved how she wasn't afraid to direct him to give her

the most pleasure. She'd done it last night in their shared dream, and he wanted to satisfy every part of her greedy body.

He scraped his teeth across her flesh, and she arched her back wanting more. He'd promised to taste her all over tonight, and he would. After he made her his forever.

He gave her one last tug with his teeth, loving her moan, and then kissed his way up her chest and to the supple skin between her shoulder and neck. She laid her head back and to the side, giving him more room to explore and find exactly the right spot.

Just above her collarbone her skin tingled in his mouth, and he knew he'd found where her body wanted to be marked.

Steele spread her legs, reached between them and stroked her pussy. She was already wet for him. "You are mine, mate. The one created for me and me alone. I give my heart, my soul, my love, and my life to you. Wear my mark and show the world that we belong only to each other."

Her eyes were liquid heat, dark pools of green and black. "Yes, Steele. Make me yours. Be mine."

He bit down, grasping her skin between his teeth and at the same time he pushed his cock into her.

Her body squeezed him tight, her muscles pulsing around him. He could hardly wait to feel her coming on his cock.

"Mmm. Steele. You feel so good inside of me."

The dragon part of himself chanted inside his head. *Mine, mine, mine, mine.*

She was his, forever.

His dragon wanted to fuck her and come inside of her. Steele wanted to make this good for her, make sure she knew how much he cherished her and her body. He corralled the animalistic need. He slowly withdrew and pushed back in, setting a slow, steady rhythm to drive her crazy.

Fleur moaned and wrapped her legs around the back of his thighs and her arms around his shoulders. He would stay this way forever if he could, wrapped in her body.

The world around them lit up with the glow from his shard and her necklace, the light danced in swirls around them, played with her flowers and blew through the trees.

With each thrust, he sunk his teeth a little deeper into her skin, the dragon pushing him to finish it, mark her, claim her. The connection between them was so evocative, and it coursed through his body, urging him to move faster, take her harder and deeper.

Joining with Fleur was so powerful it overwhelmed him. The way her body not only accepted his but needed it. Her sweet moans and the way she whispered his name. Everything before this was pure play, practice, pretend compared to this. It was as if his own soul was pouring out of him. But he wasn't losing it to her, he was sharing it, bonding the two of them together as one.

Fleur ran her fingernails over his back. "Please, Steele. More, I need… please, more."

This was exactly where he wanted her, so close to coming, needing him to push her over the edge into ecstasy. He moved his hands down, cupping her ass and tilted her body up, setting up a new angle he knew would propel her toward coming.

He thrust deeper into her, the head of his cock grazing the roof of her channel, rasping across her g-spot.

"Holy Mount Olympus, yes, yes. Gods, yes." Fleur threw

her head back, and he wouldn't be surprised if he had his own bruises from her grip on his shoulders.

He wished he could whisper in her ear, tell her to come for him, but there was no way he could remove his mouth and teeth now. After he marked her he'd spend the next few hours telling her all the dirty things he would do to her, and then he'd do them all and more.

"Oh, don't stop. I'm so close. Please make me come, Steele. Now. Make me come."

The tight grip her pussy had on him squeezed and fluttered around him. Fucking hell, he wouldn't last any longer the way she was milking him with her sweet sex. His balls gathered tight, ready to pour into her. He pounded his cock into her, out of control, and his dragon took over.

Now, she is mine.

He bit down, his dragon fangs extending, piercing her skin. The coppery taste of her blood melted across his tongue and his dragon roared out.

Both of their bodies let go, Fleur seizing around him as he pounded into her, shooting his seed deep into her, coming hard, skyrocketing into bliss.

They lay tangled together, her body still convulsing around him, holding him tight. Both were breathing hard, and Steele's mind wanted only to hold on to the warm pleasure of her body. But his teeth were still embedded in her. He withdrew his mouth and his cock at the same time.

"No, not yet," Fleur whimpered.

"Shh, baby. I'm not going anywhere." He licked over the wound he'd given her and blew a puff of Dragon's breath to speed the healing.

Before his eyes, the blood and bruising mixed and

mingled, transforming into a permanent shape that resembled a miniature version of his own dragon tattoo.

His mark.

He kissed the new symbol of their connection on her skin and made his way up her neck and to her lips. They kissed deeply, both needing to extend their connection a bit longer.

A shiver rolling across her body reminded them they were out in the nighttime forest with wolves and who knew what else roaming around. He'd claimed, marked, and made his mate come. Now it was time to protect her.

Steele raised his head, reluctantly breaking their kiss. "Hello, beautiful mate. Let's get you home and warm."

Her eyes were sleepy and satisfied, but her arms were covered in goosebumps and another shiver moved across her body. She sighed in a way he hoped to hear a thousand more times in his lifetime and smiled at him, nodding.

He sat up, pulling her into his arms and rubbed his hands briskly across her skin. There was one last thing he wanted to do before they left their mating spot. He wasn't sure how or why he knew he needed to give his soul shard to Fleur, but he knew with his entire being that it was important that he did.

Steele slipped the cord that held his soul shard over his head.

Fleur gasped and pressed the talisman against his skin. "What are you doing? The last time you weren't wearing that, you died."

"Fleur, you saved this for me once before. Will you save it for me now and forever?"

She shook her head, a panic in her eyes. "I don't understand. It's a part of your soul. How can you live without it?"

"You are my soul. Take this part of it and keep it safe, as I will keep you safe."

The shard vibrated against his skin under her fingers. Her eyes went wide and flicked between her hand and his face. She lifted her hand and the shard glowed brightly into the night. Then it floated up from his skin, reaching toward Fleur.

Fleur's own necklace lit up and drifted off her neck. "Whoa."

Steele took the small tree-shaped charm in his hand. It disintegrated into twenty or so multi-colored dragon scales that lifted into the air, swirling around his shard, drawing it from him to Fleur, and placing it around her neck.

Some of the light from the crystal flowed into the dragon mark on her skin, turning the bruising into a shimmering ink-like tattoo.

Steele's own dragon tattoo, the literal representation of the dragon part of himself, thrashed on his skin in response, absorbing another fraction of the light, and reveling in it.

The power he'd felt in the parking lot when he'd put his shard on for the first time after meeting Fleur, flowed through him again, reigniting in him.

He grabbed Fleur and held her tight against his chest. The power building inside threatened to overtake him, and his dragon pushed to the surface. Until Fleur raised her hand and stroked his cheek.

He looked down into her eyes and saw his own soul reflected back.

"Shh, dragon of mine. Your soul is safe with me," she whispered and pressed a gentle kiss to his lips.

Yes. Only with her.

Steele kissed her back, wanting to take her again, reaffirm their new lives together.

A hot whoosh of air and clapping of hands behind him stopped that idea dead in its tracks.

"That's was quite a show you two put on. A little vanilla for my tastes. I would have had her plump ass in the air, fucking her hard, dragon style, but to each his own."

Steele whipped around, pushing Fleur behind him. His dragon shimmered near the surface ready to defend and attack whoever thought it was funny to invade this intimate moment.

A man, only partly visible in the shadows, leaned against a nearby tree.

"Who the fuck are you?"

His dragon writhed under the surface, fighting to get out. Something was very wrong with this stranger. He wore no shard, and had no light in him. He didn't just slip between the shadows, he was a shadow.

Fuck. Demon.

The stranger plucked one of the many white flowers that had sprung up from Fleur's desire. She squeaked and a mountain of leaves swirled around them, covering her from the neck down and Steele from the waist.

Her layer of protection might guard them from the demon dragon's view, but not much more. This was no ordinary hellion. His human form was too real, his speech too precise and natural.

Fucking dumbass move to be so vulnerable when he knew demon dragons were in the area. He hadn't counted on any other demons. He should have taken Fleur home. His mate lust had put her in danger.

The demon sauntered toward them, twirling a jeweled dagger through his fingers. "Too bad you gave your little whore nymph that shard."

"Stay behind me." If he told Fleur to run he knew he could keep this demon occupied long enough for her to get away, but there could be others lurking. The demons must have teamed up with the demon dragons to wreak their havoc double on this land. Where were the rest of the dragon warriors? Shit.

He lowered his voice. "Fleur, do you know how to get back to the area where we met for the ritual? I need you to find the wolves or any other dragon. They'll protect you."

"Now, now, don't send her off. The others are all busy fighting or fucking. Let's just keep this between us, shall we?"

Fleur gripped Steele's hand. "I'm not leaving you to battle those things again without me."

Nope. Not gonna happen. "You must. I can't risk your life."

"Screw that. I'm not risking your life, ya dumb dragon. You're mine now."

Any last bit of doubt that Fleur wanted to be his mate disintegrated in the heat of her words. Yeah, he was dumb, for her.

He couldn't afford not to use his head and every other resource at his disposal to protect her.

"Listen to your whore, dragon. If she runs, you die. Turn over your shard to me now—"

A tree branch slapped the demon in the head, then another and another. "You can't have it, fucktard, it's mine."

That dirty mouth of hers was fucking hot, and the perfect distraction. He jumped out of the pile of leaves, ready to let his dragon out.

The creature transformed into a mac truck of a black shimmering dragon. Holy First Dragon, he was big.

Too big to be a demon dragon. Too dark and evil to be a dragon warrior.

A young green branch wrapped around Steele's waist and sprouted a barrier of leaves over him like a loincloth.

Fleur dodged the finger of dragon's fire spurted at her. She and her pile of leaves rolled behind a tree while she shouted to him. "Protect your junk. I'm fond of that part of your anatomy."

He'd like to keep his dick intact, too, and almost hated to shift since she'd been adorable trying to protect him. But shift he did.

The roar from the beast in front of him shook leaves from the trees.

Steele let the dragon part of his being loose, growing just as big as the black brute. Before he'd fully taken on the form, he lashed out with his tail, catching the demon dragon under the chin, snapping its head back.

It spit blood from its mouth, sizzling on the ground where it landed. *"I see the First Dragon has granted your powers, boy. Enjoy them while you can."*

The black dragon lifted into the air, spraying fire in a wide arc, creating a circle of flames on the ground and in the trees around Steele. It fanned the air with its wings, growing the fire, increasing the temperature to volcano hot with each stroke.

The blazing wall separated him from Fleur.

"My love, are you safe?"

"I'm fine. Got any marshmallows?" Her voice wavered the

tiniest bit, and for that alone, Steele would roast this black dragon. The flames would become his funeral pyre.

Steele should have been burning to death himself. His scales shimmered, deflecting the heat. Hells to the yeah. He'd take advantage of every new power the First Dragon had given him.

He jumped into the air, bursting through the flames and rammed the black dragon. They both hurtled to the ground back inside the circle of fire, creating a crater with their impact. Steele landed on top of the black dragon and used his size to pin it to the ground.

"Get him, Steele. Break his face."

The black dragon struggled, trying to escape. *"You've got a bloodthirsty bitch. I can hardly wait to see her scratch and claw at my demons when I give her to them."*

Steele slashed out, his claws shredding a layer of scales and exposing the flesh beneath. He didn't bother to respond to the black dragon's empty threat. No one would ever take Fleur from him. Certainly not this dirt bag.

Blood dripped from the dragon's wounds. On Steele's next swipe he'd kill this evil dragon and send its worthless stain of an existence to hell.

"Steele. Reinforcements are coming. Dragons and wolves."

The moment that Fleur yelled the black dragon snapped his teeth down over Steele's arm, crushing the bones in an instant.

"Gah." He fell back, lashing out with his tail.

The bastard rolled out from under Steele and launched into the air once more.

No way was he getting away. Steele spread his wings to

follow and the demon dragon attacked, biting and tearing through Steele's wing before he could lift off.

That sneaky-ass move wouldn't stop Steele. He clamped his own teeth around the black dragon's lower leg.

It screeched in pain, kicking, trying to get the lock of Steele's jaw off. Even with the strength of its wings, it couldn't drag a huge dragon like the one Steele had become.

Five dragons swooped down through the sky above them. The gold used the wind to propel the other four at breakneck speeds toward the battle, then followed, monitoring the air.

The blue fired off spouts of water and ice shards, putting out the fire. The two reds, Daxton being one of them, focused in on the big black beast. As soon as they got their hands on this devil, it would be nothing but a stain on the forest floor.

The final dragon was none other than Jakob Zeleny. Seeing his leader imbued him with the strength he'd thought he'd lost during the battle.

He'd be able to introduce his mate to his Wyvern, the dragon he trusted above all others to battle by his side, and the only other dragon to have a true mate.

Steele yanked on the black's leg, pulling him to the ground. *"You're mine now, evil piece of shit."*

He didn't need the reds to kill this enemy for him. He'd do it to protect Fleur, and to make his Wyvern proud. The First Dragon had gifted him with strength and size and who knew what else. He'd say thank you very much by ridding the world of another abomination.

The dirt beneath his feet swirled with green leaves and vines. They wound up his legs and filled him with more than the gifts of the First Dragon. They charged his being with love. Fleur was with him, but safe, and he wouldn't have it any other way.

"*Back to hell, you evil spawn.*"

"Not today, ignorant little green." The black dragon slipped from Steele's grip by transforming back to a human form. It darted through the fire, right toward where Fleur was hiding behind the tree.

"*Fleur, run.*"

"Ste—" Fleur's cry cut off mid-word.

Steele pushed his dragon self back inside and ran to the spot where Fleur should have been.

The only thing there was a faint green whisp of dragon's breath from where she'd been stolen.

TO HELL IN A HANDBASKET

Fleur was in hell. Maybe literally. It had to be at least a million and a half degrees in here, in the dark. Wherever here was. Hot air burned her lungs with each breath. The wall against her back was some sort of dark craggily rock, hot to the touch, and the place damn well smelled of sulfur. Or demon dragon farts. One or the other.

Where in the world, or underworld, as the case may be, was she?

She tried squinting and then opening her eyes wide to get them to adjust to the darkness. It was like one of those scenes in a horror movie where the screen was totally black, minus the creepy music. Craptastic.

Steele was probably losing his shit right about now. She tried saying his name in her mind, hoping against hope he was in his dragon form, out looking for her and would hear. *"Steele?"*

Nothing.

The tiniest of green glows emanated from her neck. The soul shard.

She grasped it in her hand and closed her eyes. The love she felt for Steele bubbled up through her, giving her strength.

Yes. Love.

How that was possible in such a short time, she didn't know, but it was true. Sure, he was sexy hot, and whoo-boy was he a rockstar in the sack, but this was something more than lust.

He was protective, even when he didn't need to be. Which she found adorable, not that he needed to know she thought so.

But what really melted her heart was the way he was strong, yet gentle, the way he was so alpha, and yet let her have control.

She'd never felt in control of anything in her entire life. Destiny had always been the one calling the shots.

Steele changed that.

No. Hold up. That wasn't entirely true. He'd shown her there was another way. She was the one who quit waiting for destiny to happen, and started making her own life happen.

That life was with Steele.

When she opened her eyes, the cave was filled with light from the shard. It surrounded her like a protective layer. The air felt cooler, and she could breathe again. Awesomesauce.

Maybe if she got up off her butt and took a proper look around she could find some way out of this mess. Fleur got to her feet and took a second to evaluate life and limb. She wasn't missing any arms or legs and the only part that didn't feel normal was where her back had been pressed against the pokey bits of the rock.

Either her captor hadn't injured her, or she was dead and

couldn't feel the pain anymore. If it was the latter she was going to kill somebody. Then they could hang out together.

She took a deep breath and coughed at the acrid smell. Okay, so probably not dead. That meant she needed to find a way out of here.

Fleur slowly spun in a circle hoping for any hint to guide her way.

Nothing to the right, nothing behind her, but aha – there, to the left a small glimmer of red.

The light from the shard faded, as if it knew danger lay ahead, and it didn't want her to be seen.

She gingerly felt her way along the wall toward the light. The red glow brightened as she got closer, and illuminated a tunnel.

Only one way out. That was never good.

No matter how hard she tried to be quiet, the rocks crunched beneath her feet, and she sounded more like a herd of garbage trucks than a stealthy escapee.

A few more feet ahead and she saw the tunnel opened into a larger cavern. There were voices in there. One dark and gruff. The other whiny and hurt her ears. Voices like these meant bad guys.

"Damn it, boy. Why haven't you taken the shard for yourself? It's the only way." A voice that could only be described as angry Mrs. Claus echoed through the chamber.

Yikes. If that was her kidnapper's mother, no wonder he'd turned out psycho.

The crash of a rock smashing against the wall shattered cranky Claus's nagging. "You think I don't know that. I already tried."

He had? It wasn't like it would have been hard to slip the cord over her head while she'd been unconscious.

"Try harder."

"It doesn't work that way." Each word was a growl. He did not like this woman.

"Then kill her," angry Mrs. Claus said.

Uh-oh.

"You're losing your mind, witch. Why do you think I didn't kill the green dragon?"

At least there was that bit of good news. Steele was alive. She would get back to him.

"You give more credence to the mating than it deserves."

Oh, yeah? The mating had meant everything in the world to her. Steele was her family, her people, her tribe. But what did psycho kidnapper think it was important?

"Dammit. The shard is useless to me if the soul inside of it is dead."

Umm. So, if he killed her, Steele would die too? No, no, no. She backed away from her not-so-secure hiding spot. If she had to dig herself a new tunnel out of that cave with her fingernails, she would.

Steele would not die because she made a dumb move and tried to get herself killed escaping.

"You don't know that, you've never—"

"Shut. Up. Now."

"Ungrateful whoreson."

"Jealous harridan."

Oh, yeah. Definitely bad guys, and also kind of whiny twelve-year olds.

What if she couldn't dig her way out? This was crunchy, hard, sharp rock. Just walking on it made enough noise. If they heard her scraping or banging on it, they'd probably come running.

Shit.

She had to go back. Maybe if they kept arguing long enough she could sneak by them.

Yeah, right.

"Give me the soul shard, and you can go."

Great big piles of stinking shit. That dark and scary voice had come from right behind her.

She'd take a deep breath and sigh, but then she'd have to smell his ass gas.

Fleur grasped the talisman that contained part of Steele's soul in it. He'd given it to her both figuratively and literally. Letting this asshat get his hands on it would be bad news bears. She turned and faced the kidnapper. What did one say to the uber bad guy of the underworld? "Bite me."

Asshat grinned, or smirked, or scowled, Fleur couldn't tell the difference. "These teeth are more than you can handle, little witch. Don't make me use them on your delicate flesh."

"I am no delicate freaking flower. Bring it on, dickwad."

Yeah. It was all bluster. She was scared out of her mind. But he didn't need to know that. He'd said he'd tried to take the shard from her and couldn't. That had to give her some sort of advantage.

Her kidnapper shook his head. "The mouth on you. My demons will enjoy shutting it up."

Demons? Like those weird black snake-like dragons at the battle outside her apartment? Not good.

Time to get the dodge out of hell. But how? The dark cave or the cavern o' bad guys were both horrible choices.

She backed away, ready to turn and sprint back to the

cave. Maybe she missed something in there, like a magical wardrobe that could transport her away from here.

Good Gods. Her best plan was playing hide and seek to stay away from asshat and cranky Claus.

"Come here." Asshat grabbed her arm and drug her out into the cavern. Holy Hades. Were those boiling pools of magma?

There were half a dozen other tunnels leading out of the cavern, but to get to most of them she'd have to recall all her best childhood skills at playing the floor is lava. Because it was.

She was never very good at that game.

Cranky Claus came up to her, totally invading her personal space bubble and tried to grab the shard. Fleur jerked away and the crone only grasped empty air.

She had the white hair and red dress, but there was no plump cheeks or cookies and milk to this woman. She had to be a thousand years old, and was in serious need of a hamburger, or two, or twelve. No wonder she was cranky.

She narrowed her eyes and glared at Fleur then down at the shard. She pointed a craggy finger at it.

"Two dragon's souls are intermingled in that shard. It is powerful. Get it from her."

Asshat scoffed. "Don't be daft, you old hag."

She waved that finger at him. "Stupid boy. Can't you see it? Her father was a dragon."

Whoa. What?

Asshat looked her up and down, a new interest in his eyes. "The daughter of a dragon. You are a rare breed."

Nope. Nope. Nope. This old witch really was losing her mind. But maybe that was her way out of here. If she could get the two of them to fight even more than they already were, then she could use the distraction to bolt to one of the tunnels.

If she didn't die in a pool of lava in the process.

She could think about the implications of what the old lady had said later.

"Your anti-Mrs. Claus is wrong. My father was a soldier." That much she knew. "I think I'd know if he was a dragon."

No, she wouldn't. Shh.

"And, if she's so wrong about that, she's probably been lying right to your face. What else has she been lying to you about? Hmm?"

"Nice try, little witch. My hag of an aunt and I are after the same thing. It wouldn't do her any good to lie to me. Now, be a good girl and give me the soul shard."

Plan A was shot to hell, literally.

She folded her arms and cocked her hip to the side, trying to look bored with the two of them. Hopefully her not-scared-of-you façade distracted them enough while her brain went on into Miracle-Gro mode to find another way out of this. "No thanks, I'll keep it. What else do you want?"

"This is not a negotiation." He took her by the arm again and backed her toward one of the lava pools. "You will give me the shard."

"I know you can't kill me to get what you want. So, stop trying to scare me." Fleur searched the cave for any sign of life. A tiny sprout, a branch, a leaf, anything she could grasp onto for help.

The asshat growled at her.

"If you don't give me the shard, you'll wish I had killed you here and now." Black claws extended from his fingers, digging into her skin. He pushed her to her knees and kept the pressure on, shoving her face closer and closer to the hot bubbling liquid rock.

Fear and adrenaline spiked through her, sucking away her breath. One touch of the magma would burn through her skin all the way to the bone in milliseconds.

The scared small part of her that had controlled her actions most of her life begged her to cry out, give in, do exactly what they wanted her to do.

She couldn't. Her life and soul were interwoven with Steele's. She pulled on his strength, the warrior part of him that would never allow this horrible creature to win.

Black scales rippled across his arm, protecting his own skin from the heat. "Give me the shard and you won't have to feel the unending pain of lava burning away at your face."

She was so close now, she should already have third-degree burns. A ripple flashed across her own skin. The shard protecting her, or something more?

Either way, she had a reprieve, allowing her mind to clear. Yes. There. She saw the one thing that could possibly save her life. She never would have seen it from any other angle, and now she had a plan, thanks to Steele.

The thread of a root pushed through the ceiling of the cavern, and it would save her life.

LOST BUT NOT FOUND

Steele tried to take to the air, and search the sky and forest for any sign of Fleur or the thing that had stolen her.

His wounds, the crushed arm and broken wing, should be healing. They weren't. His wing wouldn't move, much less allow him flight.

He joined the others searching, scanning for any sign of Fleur. Could there be any chance his flower had found refuge with another dragon or the wolves? He knew in his heart she hadn't, but he called out to her with his mind anyway. *"Fleur. Where are you? Tell me you're safe."*

Nothing. Either someone or something was blocking his connection with her, or she was too far away. A deep ache behind his heart pulsed with each second that went by without her.

How could he have let this happen?

She was his to protect, and he'd bombed. Some mate he was. The failure burned through him, blistering and scalding him with self-recriminations.

The battalion of his dragon kin arrived too late, and just in time. A horde of demon dragons popped out from behind every tree. The black dragon and Fleur were nowhere in sight.

The dragons fought this new threat, holding the horde at bay, keeping the wolves and their mating ritual safe. Steele threw his fears and frustrations into a killing rage.

One demon dragon after another fell to his teeth and claws. The bastards would die—they would all die—until he had Fleur back in his arms again.

He'd give his entire treasure trove, all his gold and jewels, all his stocks and bonds, to find her and know she was safe. No, he would give more, he would give everything he could. His fortune, his livelihood, his skills, his sanity.

His life.

An emotion he couldn't identify, so sweet and bitter at the same time, kicked him in the gut for thinking he could give his life for hers.

Their souls were intertwined, and giving up his life wouldn't save her. That much he knew. He wouldn't die for her, he would live for her. Fight for her.

A line of the dark bastards moved toward him, targeting him because of his injuries. Even with his heart torn in two he would still fight to get Fleur back. He tore through half of them with his tail. The last one in the line, he grabbed with his good arm and slammed it into a tree, holding it there by the throat.

"Where is Fleur?"

The bastard squirmed and writhed, trying to push Steele's claws away from where they were piercing its throat.

Steele didn't fucking care. It would tell him what he

wanted to know or suffer torture worse than death. *"Where is Fleur? Tell me or die an excruciating death."*

"Kill me. Never tell you, warrior shit."

Fine. Steele closed his claws and ripped the demon dragon's head from his body, tossing it toward the remaining enemy.

"Steele. Good kill. I can feel the increase in your powers. Who is Fleur and why are you asking these abominations about her?"

Jakob emulated him and tossed a matching demon dragon head at the final two demon dragons still fighting.

Thank the First Dragon. Jakob would help him find Fleur.

They stalked toward the demon dragons, who were back to back and surrounded.

"She is my true mate."

Jakob took his eyes off the prize and glanced over at Steele. One of the demon dragons attacked and without taking his eyes off Steele, Jakob speared it through the heart with the spikes on his tail.

"Your true mate?"

Steele nodded. Jakob understood.

"Ciara will be pleased to hear that. You must bring her to Prague as soon as you can. The demon dragons have her?"

The fact that Jakob simply assumed they would get Fleur back so he could bring her to meet the Wyvern's true mate too, gave Steele the hope he needed.

"I believe so. We were battling one. He was different from the others. Bigger, smarter.

Jakob slashed his tail through the trees, clearing the ground of the ash and stains of their kills. *"Strange. We need to find out where it took her and why."*

The final demon dragon screeched. The blue dragon had

its legs trapped in hunks of ice. The reds, moved in for the kill.

"*Hold,*" Jakob called out to the others.

The older red glared at him, but held its dragon fire in. Steele had never seen a red do that.

"*You'd better have a good reason why I can't destroy this thing right now, little brother.*" The thunder of the red's alpha of all alpha's voice rang through all their minds.

The big red must be Match Czervony, the red Wyvern. Dax really had called in the big guns.

"*They have Steele's true mate.*"

Every one of the dragons in the circle stared at Steele. Each were awed in their own way. Steele was still in awe himself that the First Dragon had gifted him with a true mate.

Match nodded. "*All the more reason.*"

Time for Steele to step up. "*We can interrogate it to find out where they've taken her.*"

The gold dragon shook his head. "*Good luck with that. We'd be better off killing it now and searching on our own. I'll call in one of my elite teams.*"

The same alpha tone came through in the golden dragon who had to be Cage Gylden. Fucking hell, that made three Wyverns.

Steele had been in hundreds of battles with the demon dragons and had received plenty of back-up and reinforcements from all the dragon warrior wyrs, but never had he seen three of the four Wyverns together in the same place in response to a call for help.

He stared over at the blue dragon. Could it be?

Humor danced in the dragon's bright blue eyes, and it nodded at him. Yep. Ky Puru, the blue dragon Wyvern was here. Something more than a battle with some demon dragons and a wolf mating was going on here.

Steele would think about that later. If the most powerful dragon warriors in the world were here to help him get Fleur back, he'd take it and be grateful.

Jakob circled the demon dragon, not giving it a chance to move, much less escape. *"Give Steele a chance to learn what he can. Then you'll get to have your way with it."*

Match stepped back to stand next to Daxton and waved Steele forward. *"Do your worst, young green."*

Steele's instinct was to scare the demon dung out of this dragon-like beast with pain or torture. How he would love to take it apart piece by piece for all the pain and suffering it had inflicted on the world. On him.

His claws itched to get to slice into the scales, extract what he needed to know. But that wouldn't get him anywhere. No amount of physical pain would phase something that had been spawned to do the same to humans, dragons, wolves, or any other living being.

He needed to be smart, like Fleur. Do something it wouldn't expect, like when she'd surrounded him with the vines in the bathroom. She'd gotten what she wanted even though Steele could have easily broken through. She'd made him want to give in to her wishes.

What could drive a dumb piece of shit like this into giving Steele the information he needed? Drive it insane enough to talk? Did demon dragons have other emotions? Did they hope and wish for things?

That was it.

Steele paced slowly letting the thing struggle and thrash against Jakob's tail.

"Last one standing, huh? That must make you pretty damn proud."

It spat at him. *"Fuck you, dragon."*

A complete sentence. A miracle from one of these stupid sons of a bitches. Steele could work with that. *"I suspected you were different from the other demon dragons. Better than those that are now black smudges of ash in the dirt. How did you do it?"*

"Steele, what are you doing? Slash it or I'll burn it for you. Get what you need from him." Daxton's dragon fire licked at the edges of his teeth.

The demon dragon hissed at Dax, but then looked at Steele. *"How I do what?"*

That's right. Play into my hand. *"You're smarter than the other demon dragons I've come up against. I could almost mistake you for a real dragon."*

"This piece of shit? Ha." Dax started forward but Match stopped him, holding him back with his tail.

"See, the rest of them think you're just a minion. You know better, don't you? I can see that. You're more than a mindless monster."

It's snake-like tongue flicked through the air, testing to see what it could get from the emotions Steele was working hard to keep in check. *"Yes. I better."*

"I bet you even know where they've taken the woman." Take the bait, take the bait.

"No."

Shit. *"No, I'm surprised. A smart dragon like you?"*

"No. I know better."

"Of course, you do. What do you know?"

If Jakob hadn't been holding the damn thing against a tree,

it might have been dancing a jig. *"Your woman is dead dead dead."*

Dead. Dead. Dead.

Fleur was gone? Steele's heart plummeted, spiraling into pain and darkness.

His vision went hazy, and all he saw was Fleur's smile, the way she made his soul, not just the shard, glow with all the love he had inside for her.

His soul would wither if she was dead.

They were one. He didn't understand how he knew, but Fleur was alive, because if she wasn't, he would die with her.

The demon dragon squealed, not because Jakob was twisting the spikes of his tail into its chest, but out of thrill of seeing Steele's painful reaction.

Steele was this close to stabbing the demon dragon through the eye. It was taunting him.

He shook off the possibility of the demon dragon's words being true. They couldn't be. *"That's beneath you. Too easy of a lie."*

"Easy?" It tilted its head to the side like this was the first time that word had ever entered its consciousness.

"Yes. Lies are easy. Cheap. You know what has power?" He got right up in the beast's face and whispered. *"Real power?"*

It groaned and breathed faster. *"Want power."*

"Are you sure? Can you handle it? I don't know. You're smart, but are you strong enough to handle it?"

It squirmed. *"Yes. Yesssss. Give me."*

Steele shrugged and turned his back. Denying it a little longer, making it want to hear what he had to say. *"Truth."* Steele whipped around staring at the demon dragon eye to eye. *"The truth is more powerful than you can imagine."*

It narrowed its eyes and Steele had to push the air in and out of his lungs to make sure the thing didn't get a whiff of doubt that every word was the path to pure power.

"I know truth." It paused waiting to see how that felt coming out of its mouth. *"Truth about woman."*

He couldn't get too excited. He almost had what he wanted and then he could rip its throat out. *"I don't know. You could be lying about that. Prove it."*

"Woman not dead. Yet. Woman slave to AllFather."

A slave. He would kill this all father twice. *"Who is all father?"*

"I powerful. You stupid."

Maybe he was for trying to talk to a demon dragon. But he'd gotten this far. *"I am. Show me how stupid I am. Tell me who all father is, where he is."*

"AllFather father of all demon dragons. You kill one. He fuck demon. Make new demon dragon."

Disgusting, but more information than they'd ever gotten before about the origin of the demon dragons. *"Oh, man. How did I not know? You know so much. What else? How does a demon make a demon dragon?"*

"You stupid. Demon not make demon dragon. Dragon make demon dragon."

A dragon was doing this, creating a legion of abominations. That black dragon they'd fought was more than a demon. Steele glanced at Jakob then Match. They both shook their heads indicating they didn't know what or whom the demon dragon was talking about either.

It had to be lying again.

"Huh. That's interesting. I could listen to you talk all day. So, this dragon. Where is he? I bet you know."

"*No.*"

Shit. Now it clams up? "*No? Come on. You're smart, you know.*"

"*No. AllFather go down. He hide woman from you.*"

"*You must have seen him, you know he's made the woman his slave.*" Fuck, that hurt to say. Enough was enough. Time to find Fleur. "*Down, where?*"

"*Down. You not find AllFather. You never find woman. I fuck woman.*"

Not in this lifetime or any other. Steele stabbed the demon through the eye and ripped off its head. He sliced through the entire tree the demon had been trapped on. Then stomped the trunk into the ground and smashed the demon dragon's body into the hole in the ground.

"Well, that thing is pretty damn dead." The voice of one of Fleur's friend's broke through Steele's frenzy. He stomped one more time and looked up to see a circle of men and women, all wolf shifters. They were interspersed with the dragon warriors.

The dragons shifted into their human forms, one by one, until Steele was the only one still in his beast. He took three, then five deep breaths, trying to contain the rage inside. His dragon self wanted to fly, search, tear, shred, until he had his mate back.

If he was going to find her, he needed their help.

The change finally shimmered through him, and he stood with the rest of the group. His fists were clenched, his heart and gut were eating him from the inside out, and his injuries burned, but he was human.

Jakob put a hand on his shoulder, giving him the solidarity, the knowledge that he had a support team. He didn't have to do this alone.

Match addressed the wolf shifters. "Do you have any geothermal activity in this area?"

Two of the wolf females Steele recognized, Heli and Selena glanced at each other. "We have hot springs in the area. Why?"

"Winner, winner, chicken dinner," Dax said. "Demon dragons like to live and congregate in volcanoes and other underground high temperature biomes."

Match nodded. "The stain said this all father dude went down. If it's anything like the demon dragons, the area around your hot springs would be its first escape route."

Niko stepped forward. "What can we do to keep our packs safe? The protection your warriors gave us tonight is appreciated, but you won't always be around. What if they come back once you leave?"

These people were Fleur's friends, her family even. Whatever happened, he would make sure the dragon warriors would protect her people like he would protect her.

The alpha in Match recognized the same in Niko. "We must root out their nest and destroy them so they do not plague this area."

Steele may be injured, he may have failed in his duty to protect his mate, and he may not ever be worthy of Fleur's love, but he had it, and he would put it above all else. "Not before we find Fleur."

Selena walked over and squeezed his cheek. "I knew you'd finally win her over. Let's go get your mate."

WITCHY WOMAN

Fleur closed her eyes and thought of Steele. The way he'd pursued her relentlessly. The way he kissed her and loved her. The way he'd given his soul into her care, and the way she gave hers to him.

"What are you doing, witch? Your magic can't save you."

She ignored the disdain and disgust in the demon's words. Her love was more powerful than his hatred.

She pushed every bit of that love toward the teeny-tiny root and urged it to grow. Cracks and crunches of the rock breaking echoed all through the cavern and the scent of newly turned earth and fresh growth overtook the stench of sulfer.

"A tree root is not going to save you from an agonizing lava burn."

Fleur opened her eyes and smiled at the asshat. He was wrong. The roots stretched down, creating first a wall of tangled wood between them and the creepy crone, and then a mass weaving covering the lava closest to her.

The shard at her neck glowed brightly, changing the color of the air around them from red to green.

The crone rattled the cage of branches and shouted through them. "Boy, see its power. Get the shard from her. Claim what is rightfully yours."

The man snarled and black scales rippled across his body. His hands transformed into dark claws the color of dirty oil. They swiped across her chest, shredding her shirt and cutting deep, leaving gashes that oozed black sludge.

She swallowed the scream, not wanting him to see her give into any pain he could inflict. She held fast to the knowledge that try as he might, his torture hadn't sliced through the cord of the shard.

He roared, trying to grasp the crystal. "Give it to me, whore."

"Get off." Fleur twisted and slapped at his claws. She pushed her power far beyond where she'd gone before forcing the tree roots to twice, three, four times its normal size. A chunk of the ceiling fell, breaking away and landing in great pieces all around them.

One narrowly missed the half-dragon-half asshole's head. That pissed him off even more. She'd hoped she could injure him and get him to let her go, even run away.

Nope.

He seized her by the throat with one giant clawed fist and grabbed for the shard with the other. Fleur clutched his arms attempting to save both her life and the shard.

"Never. You'll never get it."

He growled and flames licked at the edges of his mouth. "I will."

The fire burst out at her and this time she did scream, turning her head away. But the flames never touched her, didn't burn her skin.

"What the fuck? What are you?" The man shook her and shot his fiery breath at her again.

It licked across her skin, but didn't hurt any more than incredibly bad breath.

Fleur blinked. There was something different about her eyelids. Or was it her eyes? The world around her turned technicolor, sharper. The heat the shard had protected her from lessened even more and the wounds on her chest hurt less. A change was rising in her from the inside.

She glared at her captor. Thorny vines wrapped around his claws and fist, drawing blood and crushing the scales. "Hells bells, why does everyone have to ask what I am?"

She'd been asked that her entire life. Those that didn't care to ask simply shunned her. Now she was being tortured, and she still couldn't answer the question. She didn't know herself.

She'd clung to her unknown destiny her whole life, hiding behind it. She would know who she was when her fate showed up to tell her.

Screw that.

A renewed power built inside.

"You want to know what I am?" She released her grip on him as more vines and branches wrapped around them both. "You can talk to the hand. No, talk to the finger, because I'm not taking any more questions today."

Fleur raised her middle finger to the asshat's face, holding it steady and strong.

Smoke curled out of his snarl-puss face. He glanced at the shard and to her face. "There are plenty of other ways to get what I want, hundreds of dragons who don't know how precious the gift is."

He released her, breaking through the vines and dropped her to the ground. She landed close to the lava, protected only by the thin layer of roots that were burning up by the second. Still she didn't feel the heat.

"If you won't give me the soul shard, you can die and take your dragon with you."

He kicked at her, sending her careening into the lava. She raised her arms into the air, calling the plants to her. A branch stretched down, wrapping around each arm and pulling her up and away from the danger.

The man transformed fully into a black beast of a dragon and crashed through the wooden barrier. He took flight and torpedoed across the lava, following its flow deeper into the ground.

The crone screeched after him and disappeared into a puff of black smoke.

A great roar bubbled up from the direction the black dragon had flown and the earth shook below her. More of the ceiling caved in and the floor below her cracked right on cue like the set of an action adventure disaster movie.

Crapping crappity crap crap. Fleur had been ready to release a sigh of relief, but they hadn't let her escape at all. They were going to trap her underground in the cavern of death and despair.

Where was a dragon warrior when she needed one?

"He's waiting for you." The whisper of a soft feminine voice slid into her head.

"What? Hello? Who's there?"

"Go, Fleur. Quickly."

"Where? I don't see a way out." The floor shook again, and she fell. "Oh, Gods on Olympus. I'm going to die in here, aren't I? This is my destiny coming to bite me in the ass."

That would teach her to think she could ignore what the universe had predetermined her life would be.

The image of a gorgeous mother-nature diva, white flowing robes, dark hair, and plump soft curves formed before her.

For the briefest moment, she saw a reflection in the woman's eyes of herself, but instead of her own olive skin, she saw white scales.

The woman pointed toward the tunnel in the rock Fleur had come through before. The roots had opened a new path that angled up to the surface. *"Dammit, girl. Screw destiny. Run."*

She had said it. Now she was truly going to do it.

Screw. Stupid. Destiny.

She wanted to live.

The floor shook again, but this time the falling rock uncovered more roots. The tree she'd coaxed into helping her had continued to swell and fill the cavern with its tendrils. The leafy canopy of the tree must be huge above the ground.

She scrambled onto the nearest root and encouraged more growth, jumping across from sprout to sprout across the cracks in the ground and the bubbling lava.

Her muscles were on fire, and she vowed to start doing squats if her legs would get her out of here in one piece. The room was collapsing before her eyes.

She put on one final burst of speed. The white-robed woman drifted alongside of her, waving her hands and whispering foreign words.

A tremor grabbed Fleur's heart, pushing out, shimmering over her entire body. One second she was running and the next, she flew into the tunnel, the earth falling in a tidal wave of dirt and rock behind her.

Flying. Holy smokes, literally flying. She clawed at the rock to make room for her and her big ole white wings. A ginormous crack in the earth opened before her and she jumped into the air, dodging falling rocks and hot water spilling from above.

"Steele? Are you there? Can you hear me?"

"Fleur? We found your dragon tree. I'm coming."

She didn't know what a dragon tree was, but she could feel Steele, he was close.

"I'm flying up through a crack in the ground."

He was silent for a moment. *"Did you say flying?"*

"Yeah, thanks to the woman in white with me." Or, she had been. The woman wasn't beside her anymore.

The night sky with the moon and stars were visible above. Almost there. Almost back to Steele.

A great roar came from behind her and the crack widened. Fleur looked over her shoulder and saw the black dragon hot on her tail.

Between them was the woman in white.

"Go, little daughter. Hurry. I've muddled the dragon's sight. Kurjara cannot see this part of you. Get to the surface and shift into your human form."

Go, go, go. Hopefully Steele would know how to help her shift, because she didn't have a clue.

She burst out of the ground and into the sky. Several dragons were circling the biggest tree in the forest. It towered above all the others, and its branches stretched out like the wings of dragon.

She'd made a great big green dragon tree.

It was beautiful and amazing, but not as incredible as the sight of her own big green dragon pacing beneath it. "*Steele.*"

She swooped down and skidded across the ground. Her body shimmered and her feet transformed, then her legs, and torso, and arms, which she wrapped around Steele and held him tight.

He shifted instantly into his human form and held her tight against his chest with one arm. "Thank the first dragon. I failed you, my love. Forgive me."

First, she would kiss him, making sure his lips and tongue, teeth and tonsils knew how much she missed them. Then she'd set him straight on the whole failure thing.

His kissy face plans matched hers. He pressed her against the tree trunk and mashed his lips against hers, taking her in a soul-deep kiss. The moment they touched, a sense of overwhelming joy and rightness to her world flowed through, in, and around them both.

She could kiss him forever, except she knew danger was on its way. If they were going to fight it off together, she needed him to know everything that was in her heart and to heal his. He thought he'd failed her, when in reality he'd saved her, helped her save herself from living a small life.

As much as she didn't want to, she broke the kiss and pressed her finger against his lips before he could say a word. "The black dragon is coming, so let me say this before the battle." He sucked the end of her finger into his mouth, but waited for her to speak.

When this was over they were going to spend a long damn time staring into each other's eyes. In bed.

The thunder and heat of dragon fire filled the air. She had

only seconds before the black dragon and his special brand of destruction arrived.

The great tree shuddered and the ground moved beneath their feet. Steele steadied them against the trunk, keeping them both from falling.

Crap. She had a whole speech prepared, about how he was a warrior that has to protect the whole world from the evil she didn't even know existed until yesterday. That would have to wait. Short, sweet, and to the point. They had a beast to battle.

"Love of my life, you're badass. But you don't have to protect me. I think it's actually my job to keep you and your soul safe, so you can keep on saving the world."

Steele shook his head and clenched his jaw. "I am never leaving you exposed to a draft of cold air, much less demon dragons. I can't, will not, lose you again. It almost killed me to think about those things even touching you."

The black dragon surged out of the ground, taking half a ton of earth and trees with him and raining it down along with fireballs of rock and lava.

Dragons and wolves scattered to avoid the debris. Oh, no. The Troika pack was here. Her friends, the closest thing she had to a family, were in danger, too.

She and Steele had to stop the black dragon before it hurt any of them.

Fleur grabbed Steele's arms and saw his wounds weren't healing. They matched the ones across her chest.

Both were filled with a black taint, something evil and not of the earth.

White scales rippled across her arms. What was inside of

her, the part that she'd never been able to recognize or understand, pushed to get out.

"Trust me, Steele. Together we are stronger, together, we can save Rogue from the black dragon."

It wasn't only the dragon that Steele had awakened in her, but love.

The antidote for evil.

BATTLING DEMONS

*D*eep inside, Steele battled what no warrior, dragon or human wanted to admit. He was afraid.

Not the adrenaline-pumping kind of fear that he could push aside and do his job. That was easy.

How could he be the badass she thought he was?

Fleur was here, in his arms again, safe and mostly sound. She was out of her goddamn mind if she thought he'd let her out of his sight for even a second.

But then she went and asked him to trust her.

No, she hadn't asked. She'd told him to trust her.

Branches on the tree above them shattered and rained down sharp spikes of wood. Steele turned his back to deflect what he could from hurting Fleur. The shard at her neck glowed green with swirls of white interspersed creating a layer of light surrounding them both. Any projectile that got even close sizzled in the light, dissolving before his eyes.

Her eyes flicked back and forth, her gaze searching his, impatiently waiting for him to agree to put them both in harm's way.

The smart, sass mouthed, powerful woman he'd recognized in her was no longer hiding behind her destiny. She'd grown into her true self, and it was a sight to behold. If it was possible, Steele fell even more in love with her standing under that tree waiting for the world to explode, knowing if he would trust in her, they could save it, together.

He didn't understand where her absolute faith in him came from, especially after he'd flunked Protect Your Mate 101 already.

But she'd just demonstrated her new found powers to him. If she was sure, and she was, he would put his trust in her instead of himself.

"I trust you, little flower. Tell me what you want me to do."

The smile that spread across her face cemented his decision to trust her. She kissed him, sucking his tongue into her mouth, and if evil incarnate wasn't flying around over their heads he'd let her have her way with him.

She nipped his lip with her teeth and ended their three-second make-out session. "You go fight the black dragon. I'll keep you safe."

"I can't fly. The bones in my wing is broken and no matter how many times I shift into my dragon form it won't heal."

"Turn around." She spun him and pushed his shirt up revealing his broken shoulder and arm. "Why didn't you say something?"

"I was too busy holding you."

"Let me see what I can do."

"Jakob already tried his dragon's breath. It helped, but—" Fleur's breath on his skin took his words and turned them into mush. Whatever she was doing was far behind any dragon's breath he'd ever experienced. Normally it was like warm touch, but her healing power felt like Icy Hot on steroids.

She continued to blow across his skin, down his arm, her lips pursed, white mist and green dragon's breath licking over his wounds. Black oil seeped from him everywhere her breath touched giving him instant relief. The skin knitted together and the bones underneath reformed, stronger, infused with a new vigor.

She glanced up, still blowing, grinned at him, and winked.

One more part of his body went harder than it ever had before, too. "Promise me when this is over you'll use those lips on my cock."

"What do you think that wink was for?" She laughed. "Now, go. Defeat the black dragon, save my friends and their home."

Steele kissed his mate once more for luck and shifted into his dragon form, taking to the air.

The black dragon rolled through the sky, shooting jets of dragon's fire at Jakob and the other Wyverns.

Cage used his power over the wind to easily avoid the attacks, and propelled the other dragon warriors out of harm's way. But in the dark of night, he was tiring fast.

They needed to work together and move the battle to the ground, where he and Jakob could dig in and take over. The reds and Ky could use their fire and ice to destroy the legion of demon dragons pouring out of the same crack in the ground Fleur and the black dragon had emerged from.

Steele glanced down and saw Fleur's friends rapidly shift into wolves and form a circle around her and the tree.

The demon dragons attacked.

Fuck. There were so many, there was no way the wolves

could hold them at bay. Steele dove for the ground until he saw the burst of white power shoot from her hands, stunning the demon dragons.

"Fleur. They're coming. Get out of there."

The branches on the trees grew in every direction, blocking every attack. *"I got this, mate. Get the black dragon."*

The wolves took advantage of that and ripped out the throats and hearts of the beasts like the dragons had taught them to. The horde turned to mere black stains before his eyes.

Well, okay then. He'd doubted the trust he'd given to his mate in that moment and had been dead wrong.

Fleur glanced up at him and raised her hands. The world around him went white with light.

"Steele, look out," Jakob and Fleur both shouted into his head.

The black dragon and his enormous claws were centimeters from Steele's head.

"You're dead and your mate will be next."

He ducked, but there was no way he would be able to avoid the attack. He braced for the impact, praying to the First Dragon to let him keep his head.

The world shifted into slow-mo, and Steele watched the razor-sharp claws inch their way closer to his neck. Shit. He'd let himself get distracted and he was about to pay the price.

"Noooooo." A screech of tortured pain came from the black dragon, and it recoiled, snapping the world back into realtime. The ends of its claws were gone and white tendrils, like fine vines crawled up his scales.

The black dragon writhed and squirmed, trying to shake off the invader. His turn to be the one distracted.

"Go, brothers. Take it down," Steele called to all the warrior dragons to join him. They attacked. Claws, wind, fire, ice, and earth joined forces, assaulting the beast, pushing it to the ground.

It landed hard, creating a crater with its impact. There were no more demon dragons to help defend the bastard. Now it would die.

Steele dove, calling upon the earth and trees, and most importantly, his mate to join him in crushing this foe once and for all. *"Let's end this, together."*

The black dragon spread its wings, even crippled by the power of Fleur's white vines. It tried to take to the air again, jumping up and over the wolves surrounding it.

The great dragon tree Fleur had created grew even bigger, reaching out for the black dragon, making sure it's only path was down. Match, Ky, and Cage joined together grabbing at it with their claws, forcing it to drop to the ground, where Steele, Jakob, Dax and the wolf pack waited to capture and destroy it once and for all.

The wolves howled and Fleur's white magic rose around them all. It filled Steele's soul, giving him strength and courage.

He spread his wings wide, his talons ready to slice the beast throat just as it had tried to do to him. He had every confidence Fleur would protect him from any attempts at a last-minute attack.

Jakob lunged, a white light, yet not Fleur's, surrounded him, too. He used his great spiked tail to push the black dragon to the ground. It thrashed, but its actions, its snout, even its thoughts and dragon's voice were muffled by the white tendrils now encasing its head. They all heard nothing from it now, but agony.

"The kill is yours, Steele. Finish him."

"Gladly."

He drew back, putting all his might behind his move. This aberration would never plague Rogue, New York or Fleur's friends. Nothing like it would ever touch Fleur again.

He moved to strike, but stopped when a woman, older than dirt, appeared between him and the black dragon. Black acrid smoke pooled around her feet and she held up her arm to block Steele's deathblow.

"Never again," she cried. She waved her arms through the air, engulfing the black dragon and herself into smoke, and disappeared, leaving only burned ground behind.

"Who the fuck was that?" Dax asked the question they all wanted the answer to.

"Some sort of a witch, one that uses the blackest of magic." Match growled and pawed at the earth where the two fugitives had been only moments before.

"Steele. Where are you? Steele?" Fleur ran through the clouds of smoke and when she saw him, she threw her arms around his great scaly neck.

"I couldn't find you through that smoke."

Steele pushed the dragon back inside, even though that part of him was still amped up and craving the kill.

"I'm right here. I'll always be here for you."

She covered his face in kisses not even stopping when someone behind her cleared their throat. When two more someone's about coughed their heads off, she relented. Not that Steele minded them watching. He didn't care as long as Fleur was in his arms.

"Sorry to break up your love fest, but can anyone explain what that was, and do we need to be worried about protecting our pack from it again?" Niko stood, buck naked in human form with his arms crossed and his mate, Zara on his arm. At least she had the sense to put some clothes on.

Jakob shifted into his human form first and addressed the worried alpha. "It was either a demon or some form of advanced demon dragon. You all took out more of its minions than I've ever seen gathered together, so I don't think you will have to worry about them anytime soon."

Match shifted next and began pacing immediately. "I don't think it was a mere demon dragon. It had powers too similar to my own. But there is nothing in the lore about a black dragon."

Cage and Ky shifted to join the conversation. Cage leaned against the tree, using it to support him in his exhaustion. "When I have recharged in the sun, I will fly back to start searching the archives for information. I think I know a succubus who might be able to help."

"I suggest we call an AllWyr to discuss this new threat, the information Steele extracted from the demon dragon, and our new ally." Ky glanced over at Fleur.

"Me?" Fleur's head snapped to stare at Ky.

Match stopped dead in front of Fleur. "Yes, little witch. What kind of family do you come from that gives you dragon powers?"

Match's tone was dark and had a tinge of threat to it. Steele itched to step between the alpha of alpha's and his mate. He didn't only because he knew Fleur could hold her own against anyone, dragon or man.

She took his hand and squeezed it, asking for his support.

He squeezed back and pulled her closer. She glanced at him, a question in her eyes. He knew this was a sensitive subject for her. But maybe his kind could put some of her questions to rest. He nodded to her.

"I never knew my father. Do you know he was a dragon?"

"Your powers. These." Ky indicated to Fleur's arm and neck. "They are clues to your heritage. I watched as you wielded your magic. Your body shimmers with white scales. Your father was not a dragon, because there are no dragon daughters. But, there is something powerful in your past."

"But the woman in white gave me those. She's the one who transformed me into the white dragon and helped me understand how to use the love inside of me."

"The woman in white?" Match questioned.

"Yeah. Long black hair, white flowing robes. Didn't you guys see her? Come to think of it. She used those words, called me a dragon's daughter."

Match grumbled and growled. "Holy First Dragon. The White Witch. You say she transformed you? I don't believe it. There is no such thing as female dragons. Let us see your dragon form now."

Fleur shrugged and closed her eyes. The shard at her neck glowed, and white scales did in fact shimmer across her body but that was the extent of her transformation.

Steele waited in as much anticipation as the rest of the group. He knew his mate was special, but a female dragon was completely unprecedented.

"That's all I've got."

"Do your mates not take on your shifter forms when you mark and claim them?" Niko waved his arm toward the other wolf shifter couples. "All of our women were human until we mated with them."

Ky stepped in to answer. "No dragon has had a true mate in the last six-hundred years. Until now."

He pointed to Jakob. "The green dragon Wyvern was the first when he found his own white witch. We assumed it was a blessing from the First Dragon for recovering the sacred relic. But it seems to have happened again with Steele."

Steele hadn't known any of that. He hadn't done anything to deserve a gift from the First Dragon. He wouldn't question why Fleur had been brought to him but be grateful she had.

He pulled her into his arms and held her tight. He wanted to take her home and love on her. She completed him and he would do everything he could for the rest of his life to deserve her. They were indeed better together.

Match wasn't quite ready to let them go. "Steele, did you see your mate in this transformation?"

"No." Except in their shared dream. "But I talked to her too. The White Witch."

"When?" That had surprised Jakob.

"The first battle against the demon dragons. I died and talked to both the First Dragon and the White Witch in a sort of afterlife."

Jakob grasped him on the shoulder, and they exchanged a knowing glance. They had more in common than just being gifted with true mates.

Match's alpha command zinged through the air. "Steele Zeleny. You and your...mate, will present yourselves to the AllWyr council to be questioned about these supposed encounters."

Fleur extracted her arm from Steele's tight grip, and

pointed a finger at the red Wyvern. "Hey, buster. We just saved your big ole dragon butts. Have a little respect."

Man, how Steele loved her sassy little mouth. It might get them both in trouble. But he'd take it.

Jakob snorted to cover a chuckle. "Forgive him, my lady. Please accept my invitation to join me in my home. We'd like you to attend us at the AllWyr to recount your miracles."

"Miracles?"

He nodded. "I count my own true mate to be a miracle in my life. You must be, too."

Fleur grinned, and Steele saw a touch of a blush cross her cheeks. "Oh. Okay. Thanks. We'd love to."

"Steele, you'll bring her to Prague?"

"Yes, sir."

Fleur clapped. "Ooh. Prague."

"Yes, that is our home. Ciara would —what does she say— ah yes, flip her shit, if I didn't invite you. She loves to throw a party, so pack accordingly."

"My home is here in Rogue. The Troika's are…" she swallowed and glanced around at the men and women who'd fought by their side. "They're my family."

The women in the circle bounded forward, pushed Steele aside and surrounded Fleur in a group hug. They all started talking at once in a high-pitched squeal that defied human ears. The alpha female's voice rang through. "Fleur, dear. We've been waiting for you to realize how much we all care for you."

The other women hugged her one by one. "You and your dragon have to come upstate and visit."

"Yes, come over to meet the Serenity Falls pack, too. I miss hanging out with you."

"Aw, you guys mean the world to me. Even if we have to move to Europe, you'll always be my home."

Steele leaned over and spoke under his breath to Jakob. "Dude. You gotta help me out. I think the she-wolves will kill me if I try to take Fleur away from them."

Jakob nodded, looking very serious. He announced his decision to the group. "I think it best if we reassign Steele and Daxton to Rogue."

If possible the squeals of the women increased in both pitch and decibels. They might have created a new weapon of mass destruction against all eardrums.

Selena Troika clapped her hands and got everyone's attention. "Ladies, gentlemen, I propose we all meet back at the Troika's Speakeasy tomorrow afternoon. It's been a long night, and I think we could all use some time in bed."

She winked at Steele and continued, "Then we can begin our plans, ladies."

"Uh-oh. I'm not sure I like the sound of that," Niko said. "Plans for what?"

"Fleur's bachelorette party, of course."

The squeals returned and were joined by groans from all the wolf-shifter men.

"I guess that means we'll need to plan a bachelor party for you, dragon," Niko said.

Holy dragon's balls.

LOVE'S DESTINY

Fleur couldn't get Steele home fast enough. She wanted to feel every part of his body on every part of hers. Several of the Troika's offered them a ride. Steele declined.

He shifted into his dragon, plucked her up in his talons, holding her gently by the shoulders and flew up and over the treetops.

"I'm going to need a new place with a balcony so you have a place to land."

"As soon as I can liquidate some of my treasure, you're getting a home with a secluded backyard where I can make love to you surrounded by the earth and forest."

His treasure?

Dragons.

"All I want is you and maybe a garden."

"Yes. I won't be able to keep my hands off of you in a garden."

That wasn't exactly what she meant, but it sounded fun anyway.

He landed on the roof of her building, just as the sun was

starting to rise. She'd lugged half a dozen planters up here and created a tiny rooftop vegetable garden in the five by five-foot area the landlord had allowed her.

She'd been able to coax anything into growing before she'd met Steele and the White Witch, but now she could turn her little plants into paradise for them both.

Fleur waved her hands over the pots and within seconds their own little secret garden sprouted up around them.

Steele shifted to his hot-arific human form and tackled her to the grass, rolling so she landed softly on his chest. His hands were everywhere at once, stripping off her clothes and touching each new inch of bare skin.

"I need you, Fleur. God, I need to see and touch and taste you from top to toes. I can't go another moment without making you mine again."

"I am yours, but take me anyway." Fleur's hands moved as frantically as his, removing his shirt and unbuckling his pants.

He shredded hers then ripped his own off. His fingers dug into her thighs and he spread them, making her straddle him beneath her.

He slid two fingers between her legs, testing to see if she was ready. "Fuck, yes. You're wet for me already. Thank god. Slide onto my cock, baby. Ride me."

Fleur reached between them and circled his hard length with her hand. She pumped his shaft twice, before pushing him into her pussy.

Foreplay could wait. She needed him now.

"Fuck yes, Fleur. God, you feel so good." He rocked his hips, thrusting up into her, holding her hips tight so all she could do was take him.

He was rough and needy, and she loved it, because she needed him the same way.

She splayed her hands across his chest, using the position to move her body, meeting him thrust for thrust. He filled her so completely, so deeply, she didn't know where he ended and she began.

Making love to him in this frantic, demanding way pushed her body into a greedy carnal place. Her inner muscles squeezed and contracted around his cock. She was already close to coming.

"Ah, fuck, Fleur. I'm not going to last if you keep that up."

Her heart rate skyrocketed as the pleasure pooled deep in her core. "I don't want you to. Come, Steele, and take me with you."

He threw his head back and arched his back, pushing deeper into her. He cried out her name, and his hot seed surged into her.

Dozens of daisies sprung up in a circle around them, petals falling through the air as her body tensed, holding Steele tight inside of her. She sucked in one last deep breath and screamed out her orgasm.

The light from the shard around her neck joined in with the dancing colors behind her eyelids. She collapsed onto Steele's chest, his cock still hard and buried deep inside of her.

He stroked her hair and held her against his chest. His breathing was just as fast as hers. "You're so fucking sexy and hot when you come like that, riding me. I could watch you do that all day."

She giggled, so happy and content in their love. "Sounds like a plan to me."

He chuckled too and turned, putting her under him. "My

turn, baby. Let's see if I can't get you to turn this rooftop into a whole field of daisies."

His cock twitched inside of her, growing harder, filling her again.

His lips went from hers down her neck and made their way to her breast. He pulled one nipple in and sucked on it rhythmically. His hips moved to match that same beat.

Fleur lifted her legs and wrapped her heels around the backs of his thighs. Every push hit her in all the best places and a new orgasm built inside.

Not once did he stop sucking on her nipple and soon his fingers joined in, pinching and pulling in time on her other one. She moaned, the pleasure-pain pushing her higher until she was so close to coming again she could hardly breathe.

"More, more, I'm so close. More."

Instead of giving her what she wanted he slowed, taking incredibly longer strokes, biting at her nipple. He took her so much higher than before, pushing her body, but never letting her come.

"Please, Steele. I…can't. Oh, god, please."

When she was sure she couldn't take another second without exploding, Steele swiveled his hips, making her see stars. He thrust into her fast and hard while still taking long slow pulls on her breast. The counterpoint blitzed her mind and body and her orgasm crashed over her, squeezing every last bit of pleasure from her.

Her body convulsed, her muscles contracting and releasing, over and over. She flew to the highest plane of blissful nirvana and floated there, still warm in Steele's arms.

When she finally drifted back into her body, she opened

her eyes and found Steele grinning down at her. He knew he'd blown her mind.

She smiled back and stretched under him, releasing the tight grip of her legs around him. When she set her feet on the ground, his cock pressed against the inside of her thigh.

He hadn't come.

She knew how to fix that.

"Hey, dragon."

"Huh?"

"I don't know where your mind is at. But I know where mine is."

She had so much love for this man, warrior, protector she'd come to know and love. Thanks to the First Dragon and his White Witch.

"Oh, yeah, babe. Where's that?"

"In the gutter." She waggled an eyebrow at him. But suddenly Steele looked so damn serious.

Uh-oh. What was wrong?

Steele kissed her gently. "That's my favorite place for it to be, babe."

She skimmed her fingers over his back. "Join me there?"

He sat up and positioned her in his lap so they were face to face. "I will. But there's something I want to ask you first."

"Okay. But don't worry. I'm not going to make you sleep in the bathtub again." She was trying to lighten the mood. It wasn't working.

"Fleur." Steele cleared his throat. "I love you with every fiber of my being. I feel like I've known you my whole life. But I don't know if it's the same for you."

He looked so vulnerable, wondering if she had the same feelings he did.

She didn't understand how, but everything they'd been through in the last, could it really be less than two days, they'd formed a bond deeper than she'd ever imagined she could have with another being, human or shifter.

She took his face in her hands and made him look at her, understand what was in her heart. "This whole mating thing pushed against every fear I've had about where I am in my life and what I thought was supposed to happen."

Steele placed his hand over hers on his cheek. "I'm sorry, baby."

"Don't be. I'm glad it happened. My whole world has flipped, turned upside down, and thank goodness. I've been fighting against you and myself since the minute you walked in my door dressed as a fireman stripper. But I'm done."

He searched her eyes. "What are you saying, Fleur?"

"I'm never again living in fear. I can and will make my own decisions in life, take responsibility for being who I truly am. You helped me find that part of me. It was buried so deep inside."

"No more waiting for your destiny?"

"Nope. I am me, and destiny can shove it. Who needs it when I've got you?"

Her life and her choices were her own, and she would take responsibility for them and their outcomes.

"I'll do everything I can, every day to be worthy of you."

"You shut that sexy dragon mouth. You don't have to work for my love. I give it unconditionally to you."

Steele pulled her hands from his face and clasped them in his. Then he moved so he was kneeling before her. "Fleur, my little flower, you've brought a magic into my life I never dreamed could ever exist. When I met you, I thought being a dragon warrior was the extent of my fate. You might not know what your destiny is supposed to be, and I'll be there to help you find it if you want. But I know mine. It's you."

Tears bubbled up in Fleur's eyes. She opened and closed her mouth three times trying to find something to say. She had no words.

"Shh, baby. I don't need you to say anything, but one word. I will be by your side forevermore, the mark you wear forever shows the dragon world that you are mine. Will you marry me and let the rest of the world know, too?"

She still couldn't talk, but she could nod her head. Flowers burst up out of the floor, roses, and lilies, and orchids, and even a few daisies.

Steele pulled her down and kissed her until they both wanted more.

"Yes. Yes, Steele." Fleur knew then she'd found her true destiny. Her true mate.

Here's a fun-sized story for the Dragons. Read about their first Halloween party in Book 2.5 - Unmask Me.

Find out what happens next in the Dragons Love Curves series in Book 3 – Bite Me.
Click here to get yours now!

ALSO BY AIDY AWARD

Dragons Love Curves

Chase Me

Tease Me

Unmask Me

Bite Me

Cage Me

Baby Me

Defy Me

Surprise Me

Dirty Dragon

Crave Me

Dragon Love Letters - Curvy Connection Exclusive

Slay Me

Play Me

Merry Me

The Black Dragon Brotherhood

Tamed

Tangled

Twisted

Fated For Curves

A Touch of Fate

A Tangled Fate

A Twist of Fate

Alpha Wolves Want Curves

Dirty Wolf

Naughty Wolf

Kinky Wolf

Hungry Wolf

Flirty Wolf - - Curvy Connection Exclusive

Grumpy Wolves

Filthy Wolf

The Fate of the Wolf Guard

Unclaimed

Untamed

Undone

Undefeated

Claimed by the Seven Realms

Protected

Stolen

Crowned

By Aidy Award and Piper Fox

Big Wolf on Campus

Cocky Jock Wolf

Bad Boy Wolf

Heart Throb Wolf

Hot Shot Wolf

Contemporary Romance by Aidy Award

The Curvy Love Series

Curvy Diversion

Curvy Temptation

Curvy Persuasion

The Curvy Seduction Saga

Rebound

Rebellion

Reignite

Rejoice

Revel

WHO LOVES DRAGONS?

A letter from the author~

Dear Reader,

Phew. This story was one wild ride. But I have to tell you, I think this might be my favorite story ever. (Okay, I say that every time I write a book. But don't tell the other books.)

Hey, would you mind leaving a review? Your opinions will be helping other readers discover my curvy girl stories, too.

Next up in the Dragons Love Curves series is a fun-sized novella called Unmask Me, where Ciara decides to throw a Halloween party for the dragons.

Remember sexy Ky, the Blue Dragon Wyvern? He is in for one hell of a ride in the next full-length novel, Bite Me. Including going to Hell and back. His heroine, Jada. Well, let's just say, she's not exactly a good girl. But she does have a thing for donuts.

There's sneak preview of chapter one from Bite Me on the very next page. So, read on!

Want more romances with curvy girls and hot alpha males?

You met the Troika Wolf pack in this story and they have their own series too! Get binge reading those sexy shifters finding their cute and curvy fated mates in the Wolves Want Curves series!

Want to get notifications when my new releases hit the shelves?

Sign up for the Curvy Connection and to say thanks for wanting to hang out with me, I'll send you *a FREE Gift ebook* right away!

Plus, I've got a present for all my elite readers.

Your very own Curvy Love Adult Coloring book!

You can also find me on me on my website www.AidyAward.com

And on all kinds of social media!

Facebook: www.facebook.com/AidyAward

Facebook Reader Group: www.facebook.com/groups/AidysAmazeballs

Twitter: @AidyAward

Instagram: www.instagram.com/AidyAward

Pinterest: www.pinterest.com/AidyAward

Goodreads: www.Goodreads.com/AidyAward

Hugs and Kisses,
--Aidy

AN EXCERPT FROM BITE ME

Too Many Demons, Not Enough Donuts

Too many demons in the kitchen spoils the soup. Or in this case donuts.

A batch of carbtastic sugary bombs of deliciousness sizzled away in the fryer, while Jada dreamed of all the decadent toppings she would put on them.

Chocolate frosting, check.

Maple cream, check.

Rainbow sprinkles. Ew, gross.

Toffee chunks. Yep.

Caramel drizzle, double check.

Some B positive, AB neg, or how about some good ol' O universal? Hells to the no.

That's what Leon wanted. It was what he always wanted. But, not only for himself. For her too.

Her father shouldn't be in the kitchen of the summer rental harassing her anyway. He didn't even like sugar or cooking or kitchens. He didn't like anything but sex and blood.

The scent of vanilla and cinnamon wafted through the air and smelled almost as good as the humans Jada waiting in the great room.

The rest of her coven was already playing with their prey. Seducing and taunting, testing and tasting, picking out the right one to satisfy their darkest urges.

The men and women Leon had lured to the ocean-side mansion were wanting and willing. A night of sexual carousing with the most sensual summer residents of the Cape was enough to tempt these unsuspecting humans to their doom. That and Leon's hypnotic incubus allure.

Jada smelled their growing arousal already. Its dark, rich, deliciousness sang to her core.

Her heart jumped, racing to catch up with the others.

A pulsing beat pushed between her legs.

Her mouth watered.

She wanted to sink her teeth into... a donut. Pure chocolate glaze running down her throat, hot and sweet. She'd take the sugar high over blood lust all day, every day, twice on Sundays.

It was the little lies she told herself that got her through the days and long, long nights.

"Jada, why do you waste your time on these human treats when there are so many delicious humans to be our treats?"

God damn it. A few more minutes and the most perfect batch of her yumtastic feast would be ready. "Go away, Leon."

He propped himself against the kitchen island and crossed his arms. "Now, now, is that any way to talk to your maker?"

As if he cared how she spoke to him. He only cared that

her absence from the nightly orgies was sowing discontent amongst the coven.

He could take his fatherly disapproval and shove it up his donut hole.

"I'm not going to your Bacchanalia. Not tonight, not ever again. I'm done with human blood."

"Yes, yes. You say that every few years." He cracked his knuckles one by one. "And are you done with the pleasures their flesh brings you too?

Sex.

She'd had enough of it to last most succubae a lifetime, or two, and she was only half demon. But, she wanted more, all the time. Sex was going to be a hell of a lot harder to give up than the blood.

The kitchen timer dinged, and Jada ignored Leon's question in favor of flipping over each of the half dozen beautifully browning cake donuts, revealing their perfectly fried underbellies. As soon as they cooled, she would smother them in rich chocolate ganache and sprinkle with chocolate chip cookie crumbles.

Three of those and a glass of milk to dunk them in were better than sex.

Almost.

"You can ignore me, fruit of my loins, but you cannot deny your true nature."

"Ehhhh." She made a sound like the buzzer in a Q&A game. "I can, and I will. Thanks for playing. Bu-bye now."

She flipped him the bird and turned to the refrigerator. He was getting to her and he knew it.

So what if she'd tried to give up human blood before? This time she had a better plan.

Replace sex with food. Replace blood with… well she hadn't figured that part out yet.

No way she waiting long enough to glaze the donuts. Chocolate milk would have to cool them off. She'd risk burning her tongue, the roof of her mouth, and her esophagus.

"If you won't come to my little party, I'll simply have to bring it to you."

The bastard wouldn't.

She ripped open the fridge door and accidentally crushed the carton of milk in her fist.

"Come in, young man. I want you to meet my daughter."

Oh hell. Leon's allure had every spark of arousal firing out of this victim. It wrapped around her and slipped into her mouth and nose. The prey was horny and hard already.

That pulsing between her legs picked up a new faster, deeper rhythm. A shiver snaked across her chest and shoulders.

Her fingers dug into the milk container and the liquid dripped down her hand. She was not beneath licking chocolate milk off her arm. Anything to quash the mouthwatering scent of the human man standing behind her.

"Let me help you with that, luscious vampire mistress." The guy's deep voice seeped into her ears. He took her wrist in his hand and pulled it back, raising it to his mouth. The second his lips touched her, a zing of pure need rushed through Jada, hitting her right behind the heart. Her fangs extended, ready to taste his pleasure.

Pleasure and pain. What this guy offered her was both.

She wanted him.

She needed him.

Even more than sugar, sweets, or even breathing. He would take her body, not understanding that she was taking his life. The sex would be phenomenal, and then he would die.

Because Jada couldn't control herself. She would make him come, sucking up his sexual energy and then she'd drink his blood until there was only a husk of the man left.

He would taste better than Dunkin, Krispy, Horton's, and Voodoo combined. The essence of his life would re-energize her, renew her, make her whole again.

Jada was so, so empty.

She'd tried for weeks to fill the gaping black hole inside of her with every comfort food the restaurants on the Cape could deliver to her. She'd tried for years to ignore the wounds her very existence continually slashed on her soul.

The only thing that came even close to the high sex and blood gave her was mounds of sugar.

She understood how millions of Americans were literally addicted to the stuff. It lit up all the right parts in the mortal half of her brain.

Not in the same way as the aroused naked man licking his way up her arm.

Maybe just one taste.

She'd be able to stop this time.

Only a little blood. If she kept the emotions buried, the human part of her that came with sex, she'd be able to control herself, only take what she needed, less if she really concentrated.

Jada let the guy kiss her shoulder, then her neck. His cock was pressed into her side, hard and ready for so much more. Lust and need poured out of him.

It was seductive, delicious.

No, blood only.

No sex.

No emotion.

It was the only way to control herself. Leon had been trying to teach her that for years.

She turned in the man's arms and he pushed her up against the refrigerator. She didn't even mind the handle jabbing her in the back. That didn't matter. Only the sexual energy pouring out of him and into her.

The scent of his carnal nature taking over was overwhelming her.

No. She wouldn't take any of it from him.

Not tonight. Not ever again. She wouldn't allow it.

"You vampires like it rough, don't you?" He shoved her hands up over her head and bit at her neck, pretending to be something he wasn't.

Another foolish human, falling prey to the legend of the vampire, not understanding the truth behind it.

Thousands of years of demons. Exactly like her.

The sting of his teeth and the way he sucked at her flesh was far from the violence she'd do to him. But, not before he got his rocks off. That made the blood, the energy, the kill so much sweeter.

Jada shifted her hips and wrapped one leg around his waist. He was so ready to go that she didn't even need her own hypnotic allure. He took her bait and began thrusting against her, dry humping her like he was made for it.

How she wanted to strip her yoga pants off and shove his hands, his mouth, and his cock between her legs.

She turned her head to the side and closed her eyes, pushing away any thought of her own pleasure. This had to be enough. This was the only way she could keep it together, keep him safe.

The rest of the humans were likely already dead. Sucked and fucked to death.

Murdered by the demon hunger.

A couple of deep breaths and she was able to open her eyes again. That was a mistake. It put Leon into her line of sight. Disgusting.

His chin was tipped up and he breathed the sexual energy in from across the room.

Didn't matter that he was her father, that it was ten-levels-of-hell wrong to be watching her and this man together. None of that meant shit to him. All Leon cared about was siphoning the lust pouring off the man as he humped her leg. That's what an Incubus King did.

Enough.

Jada yanked her hands from the man's grasp and grabbed his head. Saliva dripped from her fangs. She pushed his head sideways and scraped her teeth across the artery in his neck. The blood vibrated under his skin, calling to her.

He groaned and lost his rhythm, thrusting at her frantically. "Yeah, baby. I'm close. Bite me. I'm gonna come."

She already tasted the edge of his orgasm, hot like the most intense spices. She wanted more.

The evil inside of her needed more.

Jada sunk her teeth into his neck and sucked the first drops of blood down like the finest wine.

"Fuck, oh, fuck. I'm coming. Ahhh."

The spicy flavor of his blood and orgasm shot into her cells. She went from sipping to gulping. Taking everything she could from him.

"Yes, Jada. Take him. He is so delectable." Leon crooned his own gratification.

He was more than delectable. He was life.

The man's head lolled to the side, and still she drank. She wasn't yet satisfied. He could give her more.

A squawking beep beep beep jumped into the room, invading her consciousness, making her cringe at its assault of her ears. Wisps of acrid smoke circled the air and the scent of burned sugar permeated the room.

The donuts. She'd forgotten the donuts.

Thank god.

She pulled her teeth from the neck of the man, and he slumped in her arms.

"Hey, hey. Buddy, uh, dude." Shit, she didn't even know his name. She slapped his cheek, trying to rouse him. He fell to the floor in a giant heap.

The muscles in Jada's chest contracted, pulling tight around her heart.

No, no, no. She'd killed him. Killed another one.

Fuck. She should have known better. She'd never been able to control herself before. What made her think she would be able to stop this time? Donuts?

They might be manna from heaven, but she was from hell.

The man at her feet groaned.

Holy shit. He was still alive.

Jada dropped to the floor and patted his chest. His skin was clammy and much too pale. "Hey, guy, hey, wake up."

"Don't be stupid, Jada. It's too late. Finish him." Leon towered over her. His skin was flushed, in so much contrast to the man near death.

Leon stretched his arms wide and smiled like he'd woken

from a long-needed nap. He'd enjoyed every minute of the act that made Jada now feel sick to her stomach.

Deeper than that. She felt sick to her soul.

She couldn't do this, couldn't keep on killing. It wasn't right. She wasn't right.

The revulsion bubbled up, burning the back of her throat, until she couldn't hold it in any longer. She bolted to the sink and hurled into it.

Red blood splashed against the shiny steel.

Never again.

"Why do you insist on torturing yourself? This is who you are, little girl. This is what you are. Why are you always fighting it? After all these years, I'm growing tired of your antics."

Three hundred years. Countless lives lost so that she could live.

There had to be something more out there. In the past few months, a change worked inside of her, tugging at her psyche, pushing away the banal existence she led. It made her want that something more from life, more than death.

The empty pit in her stomach widened. She could never have whatever it was.

Without responding to Leon, she rinsed the blood down the drain and walked to the kitchen door.

"Leave now, and the life you spared will be no more." Her father's tone darkened, the demon snarl dominating his statement.

If she left, Leon would kill the man. If she stayed, Leon would kill her. Not directly, not by force, but by an eternity of his twisted form of preservation.

Jada saw that now. She would never be able to resist the call of sex and blood, and Leon would never let her.

Pure demon was what he was. No emotion, no compunction about killing innocent humans he lured to their deaths.

Taking more lives would kill her, but so would not taking them. At least if she left, she could make the choice of who and when and maybe how much.

If she couldn't leave, there was one last life she could take and end it all.

Being half human had to have some advantage.

Guilt clawed at her for leaving the guy to the mercy of Leon and her brothers and sisters. She would regret not getting away from the coven even more so.

She'd gotten as far as the kitchen door. Now, all she had to do was walk through it and out of this way of life. But, she was afraid. Without a coven, without Leon she would have no one. A succubus on her own was a dead succubus.

Dead inside or dead.

She took one step.

"I'm talking to you."

She didn't care or she didn't want to Not anymore.

"You walk away from me, and I won't be able to protect you." Leon's voice was somewhere in between pissed and concerned.

She kept going into the hallway, and up the stairs. Leon followed her all the way to her bedroom door. She tried to slam it in his face, but he caught it.

"I don't need your protection. I'm a big girl vampire now." She said the taunt in her best snotty little kid voice. Leon loved to play into the façade humans had invented to explain their kind.

"You have no idea, Jada."

Nice threat. She folded her arms and rolled her eyes at him. He always hated that. She was the only one of his offspring who wasn't in awe of him, who didn't think he hung the moon. It was one of the only things she still liked about herself.

He grinned, the evil inside making him look more creepy than happy. "You're being hunted."

Haunted was more like it. She tapped her foot. The more she annoyed him, the sooner he'd leave her alone.

"Demon dragons have attacked our coven a dozen times over the past few months, and we've kept you in the dark about it, and thus safe."

Demon dragons. After her. "What are you talking about?"

Demons didn't attack each other. Each faction was focused on what they needed from humans. They had enemies of their own to worry about. Hunters tried to destroy the children of Lilith and dragons warriors kept the Black Dragon's plague at bay.

Leon studied her face and pushed at her consciousness to see if her reaction to his news was genuine. "What is bringing this resurgence in your reluctance to connect with the coven?"

Jada shifted from one foot to the other. This was an old fight between the two of them. Leon never got why she wasn't like the others.

He narrowed his eyes. "I sent Portia to the continent to keep her from telling you about the demon dragons. May she finally learn her lesson about being loyal to coven and not the individual."

Jada wished she had that same ability to know when

someone wasn't telling her the truth. She'd inherited a lot of Leon's abilities, but that wasn't one of them. She'd have to guess. "You're lying to keep me here."

"I'm not. Ask your sister when she returns. She's fought off more of the beasts than anyone else. Leave this house and risk your life."

Jada's life wasn't worth much anyway. Maybe death by demon dragon was the way to go. Her only regret was leaving Portia behind. She was the only other person in the coven who ever understood.

Hopefully, her sister would understand her decision to leave too.

"I think I will."

Leon shrugged. "Fine. I'll be here when you need to come crying back to daddy."

Ew.

Jada shoved some of her favorite clothes into a bag, grabbed the money she'd been hoarding to buy human food, and searched around until she found the courage she'd been lacking for hundreds of years.

Succubae didn't survive on their own. That's why they formed covens under the succubus or incubus who created them.

The fastest way to kill a succubus wasn't a stake through the heart, or daylight, or garlic, like in the misinformed legends. It was banishment.

She'd basically banished herself.

Hell's big sweaty balls.

Jada hit the street running. Okay, not actually running. That would require moving her muscles more than her jiggly butt was capable of doing. Too many donuts. She did hurry along though.

Without a coven, she had no place to stay, no place to eat.

Except the donut shop out by the golf course but, it didn't open for a few more hours. Like eight.

It would take half that long to walk there anyway.

"Hey, baby. Where you going? Need a ride?" A convertible filled with horny twenty-somethings pulled up beside her.

She kept on moving, even though she could live off their combined sexual energy for a week. "No, you need a swift kick in the ass?"

"Whatever fatty." The car screeched away, the gaggle of dickheads laughing like they'd told the funniest joke ever.

Sigh. Jada had ninety-nine problems, but her curves weren't one.

That very minute every single one of those problems showed up.

Appearing out of the shadows, demon dragons formed into their black slithery snake-like forms around her.

"Alone?" one of them hissed . The sound of its voice creeped her the hell out.

Jada backed away, only to find another one right behind her. She held out her hand, like that was going to keep them from killing her. "No, my coven is, uh, meeting me here. So, you'd better get away from me."

"No." The beast in front of her sniffed the air. "No demons here. Only you."

Well, shit. She was completely defenseless. The only weapons she'd ever had were her teeth and her hypnotic allure. But it was to attract prey, not keep from being prey.

Demons didn't fight with other demons, and humans were food, not threats. She had never needed to defend herself.

"I know kung fu." More like kung food. She raised a fist in the air and took a Karate Kid stance. Her fangs extended, responding to the adrenaline coursing through her. She might not know anything about self-defense, but she could bite their faces off.

Hopefully, they wouldn't taste as bad as they looked. She wasn't into blackened lizard-skin.

The demon dragons snarled and launched into the air coming at her. She ducked and rolled, narrowly missing the outstretched claws.

There was a tree ten yards up the road. Maybe she could scramble up it. What, like demon dragons couldn't climb? She made a mad dash for the tree anyway.

A quick glance over her shoulder showed them closing in on her. Then a great flame burst out over her head and the demon dragons went up in flames one by one, squealing and dissolving into black smears of ash on the ground.

"That was a close one, dear. We almost didn't find you in time."

Whoa. A woman, in a white flowing dress straight out of the Renaissance festival, sat in the tree above her.

Beautiful didn't even begin to describe her. Long flowing dark hair, gorgeous olive skin, rosy cheeks, and a Mother Nature vibe made her absolutely stunning.

For a moment, Jada suspected the woman was a succubus. She was that good looking, that sensual. But a succubus's allure didn't work on one of their own kind.

Had she burned up the demon dragons? Jada didn't see a flame thrower anywhere.

"Uh, thanks? I thought those creepazoids were going to kill me."

The woman climbed down out of the tree, in a floating, graceful sort of way. "I'm rather fond of the term, douchecanoe. My husband says I've got a potty mouth, but secretly he likes it."

No succubus Jada had ever known had a husband. Her kind didn't mate. This lady wasn't a mere human either. Being afraid would probably be the smart thing to do. She wasn't though.

An aura of comforting, nurturing, motherly vibes surrounded the woman in white. A sensation Jada hadn't known for a long time. It hurt.

The emotional ping from her brain sent spikes of pain to her chest and settled deep in her gut. Ouch.

Hell, she was so broken.

The woman walked around Jada, or rather floated as if the wind gently carried her. "I've got something for you."

"You do? That's kind of weird."

"I've been waiting for you to leave that house, those demons, so I could give it to you."

Stalker much?

See, should have been scared.

Jada took several steps back. She was wearing tennies and yoga pants that had never been to yoga, and the woman in white had that voluminous gown on. If she didn't have to go far, she could outrun her. "Thanks again, but, I'm gonna go now."

"Here." The woman held out her hand and let a necklace with a glowing charm, hang from her fingers.

Jada couldn't take her eyes off it. She reached her hand out to touch the shining object, mesmerized by its light.

"Let me put it on you."

Jada nodded, knowing that was the best idea she'd ever heard. She bowed her head and the woman slipped the necklace around her neck, chanting a few words.

The second the charm hit her skin, Jada's world exploded into the light of a thousand suns. It blinded her and knocked her on her butt.

She couldn't breathe, couldn't move, only feel. An energy more powerful than sex and blood zipped through her, changing her from the inside out.

It completely overpowered her until darkness crept in around the edges of her consciousness. Damn it all to hell. She was going to pass out, and then who knew what this woman would do to her.

The woman knelt next to her in the grass. "Don't worry, Jada. You'll be fine. Even better when he finds you."

Another figure loomed behind the woman. Bigger, with an entirely hungry, masculine, alpha energy. He was going to eat her, she just knew it.

Instead he spoke. "It had better be soon. Kur-Jara is on the move."

Jada tried to scream or get away or even move her eyes. She couldn't.

The woman in white touched Jada's brow, strengthening the darkness, taking her consciousness. "I know. But Kaiārahi will come for her. He won't be able to resist. And this time, I added a little protection spell, so the little white witch won't connect to it for a while."

"I love your cunning mind, my heart." The man picked Jada

up like she was a little butterfly. "Come on, let's get her to Ninshubur before any of those Galla dragons or the demons she surrounds herself with stumble upon her."

The rest of her kidnappers' conversation faded along with the light and the remainder of her awareness. She could only pray she woke up again tomorrow.

The scent of coffee, frosting, and freshly made baked goods permeated her brain, and Jada sat straight up in her bed.

No, not her bed. Not her room. Not her anything.

Curtains were drawn across the windows, but sunshine leaked in and shined a spotlight a tray on the bedside table. A steaming pot of coffee, three donuts, and a note sat there.

She grabbed a donut, sniffed it, and bit in. Mmm. Sugar. A blessing from the gods. Then she picked up the note. It had only one line.

Always be yourself, unless you can be a dragon, then be a dragon.

Was that supposed to be inspirational?

Grab Bite Me to read Ky and Jada's story now!

ABOUT THE AUTHOR

Aidy Award is a curvy girl who kind of has a thing for stormtroopers. She's also the author of the popular Curvy Love series and the hot new Dragons Love Curves series. She writes curvy girl erotic romance, about real love, and dirty fun, with happy ever afters because every woman deserves great sex and even better romance, no matter her size, shape, or what the scale says.

Read the delicious tales of hot heroes and curvy heroines come to life under the covers and between the pages of Aidy's books. Then let her know because she really does want to hear from her readers.

Connect with Aidy on her website. www.AidyAward.com get her Curvy Connection, and join her Facebook Group - Aidy's Amazeballs.